THE COMPLETE TRILOGY

A FALLING STARR

FoxTales Press

DANI HOOTS

Forgotten

Angela Starr. I looked at my Portland Community College student ID, wishing the name would ring a bell. Over the past year, I had repeated the name over and over again, but nothing ever came back to me. One year ago, I woke up in a hospital with no recollection of who I was. The police performed an investigation but found nothing —no records, no family, no friends. Nothing. There was a lot of paperwork, I mean a lot, but I finally received an identity with the name they found on me. Now I am going to a community college to obtain my GED.

Since they couldn't find any info on me, and doctors weren't sure what my true age was. My counselor, Dr. Mandy, and the detective who accepted my case, Mr. Johnson, decided it would be best for me to go to a community college. They wanted to make sure I obtained the education needed before going to a university or getting a job. I tested out of a few subjects and was able to start at the college level for physics and math, but I didn't test well in English or history. When I first woke, I was speaking a different language. I could converse in English, but very little. Strangely, no linguist or specialist knew what language I was speaking. After talking to many, many people, the psychologists decided it must be part of the amnesia—that my mind had created its own language. I also knew practically no history, which could go with the disassociation thing the specialist talked about. I still could speak the other language and thought in it and wrote in it, but no one else understood it.

It aggravated me that none of the exercises or therapies the doctors gave me helped me remember at all. I still remembered nothing of my past and I started to doubt I would ever recall. I tried my best to keep on going each day, but the bitter truth was always in the back of my mind—I may never remember who I was.

"Here you go, miss." The cashier handed me my

textbooks. She looked the same age as me, whatever age that was. She wore round glasses and had short black hair and freckles.

"Thank you." I grabbed the books, each one seeming to weigh five pounds or more, and stuffed them into my backpack as the next student in line stepped forward. I wondered how students lugged such heavy bags around all day. Hoping things got easier as the school term progressed, I flipped my bag onto my back, brushed my scarlet hair behind my ear, and headed out into the crisp outdoors of the Pacific Northwest.

I had just enrolled in winter quarter and was excited to start my more intense classes, as I had completed the English for Speakers of Other Languages program. My first class of the term, WR 121: English Composition would start soon and after that I would attend PHY 122: Stars and Stellar Evolution. To be honest, I was more excited for the physics class, as astronomy, I discovered, was my favorite subject to study.

I checked the time on my watch. It had a cute little fox on it which made me smile each time I looked at it. Most everyone seemed to use their phones for checking the time instead of having a watch. Although I had a flip phone, I usually kept it powered off at school. It wasn't like I had anyone that would contact me, other than my therapist Dr. Mandy, whom I didn't enjoy talking to, anyway. So, I just kept it on me for emergencies and checked it when I got back to my apartment.

I had half an hour to get to my class, which was plenty of time. After taking a few steps forward I realized I didn't know which building and classroom it was in. I pulled out my class schedule to find it was in CA TH 204. Clear across campus. Letting out a slight groan, I folded the paper and stuck it in my pocket. Good thing I had my umbrella as it started to rain. Again. I knew once I finished classes here, I would move to somewhere sunnier, like California or something similar. I hated the rain, it made walking around the city almost unbearable. A little was fine, but downpours were horrible. I wanted to be somewhere it was almost always sunny, and in a big city.

Having all my textbooks in my bag did not help my hatred for having to walk in the cold, wet weather. My back was already hurting, and I would still have to walk home later. Although most of the way to my apartment was by taking the yellow line for the MAX, the Metropolitan Area Express light rail, it was still a few more blocks of walking that I wasn't looking forward to.

I glanced around at other students as they made their way to their own classes. I speculated what their lives were like, who they were as children, if they knew their families, if they had any friends—whether they left their books at home or not. A knot tightened in my stomach. I always regretted it, but I couldn't help from feeling jealous. It didn't hurt as much as it used to, but, every once in a while, it ate me up inside.

I noticed a tall blond man walking toward me. He opened his mouth as if he wanted to call out. I thought he must have recognized someone behind me—that was the only reason he'd be looking my way. I peered behind me to find a group of girls. He probably knew one of them, as they looked like the type of girls that knew everyone on campus. I turned back to find him still examining me. My cheeks blushed as I didn't know how to respond nor knew if he was really looking at me or someone else. Keeping my head down, I kept on walking. I didn't want to seem like an idiot— like when someone waves and you wave back to only find they were waving at someone else. I had done that way too many times. Besides, I didn't know anyone on campus. Or anywhere, for that matter.

He said nothing as I passed him, almost brushing his shoulder. He smelled... familiar. Woody, with a hint of fruit, but nothing I had ever smelled in Portland. I stopped dead in the middle of the pathway.

I knew that smell. I knew that face. Those blue eyes, shaggy hair, and a five o'clock shadow that never seemed to leave his face no matter how often he shaved. Mick? Nick? I could see him in my mind, smiling, laughing. Did I find someone that I once knew?

I spun around, but there was no trace of him. I shook my head and tried to forget it. There was no way I knew him. I wasn't ever that lucky.

As I started back toward the classroom, my head began to pound. I stopped for a second and grabbed my head. It hurt bad—unlike any other headache or migraine before. After a few moments, the pain began to dull, but lingered a bit. That's all I needed on the first day of class.

Checking my watch again, I found that fifteen minutes had passed already and my heart began to race, even though I knew I would probably not be late. I hated being late, it was one of my fears, even though most professors showed up late. I was punctual, as my therapist put it, however she never was. Her appointments always went over and it bugged me a lot.

I kept an eye out for the blond guy I had seen earlier, but didn't see him anywhere. There were around 20,000 students at this campus location alone, so I doubted I would run into him, but anything was possible I supposed. I didn't know what I would do if I saw him though. How would I even ask "Hey, I don't have any of my memories, can you tell me if we have known each other in the past?" No, that would be too awkward. He probably just remembered my face from when it was on the news. Some people commented and asked me about it. I usually ignored them.

I made it to my classroom with ten minutes to spare. Getting a seat at the front of the classroom, I pulled out my notebook and textbook. That was all I needed at the moment. Leaning back in my seat, I took in the surroundings. The small group of 27 people were a mix of students of all different ages and cultures. Most had their computers open, some on Facebook or getting their notes ready; mainly the former. I had a Facebook profile, as most students did to keep informed about things happening around campus and for working on group projects. I also owned a laptop but I didn't enjoy taking notes on it. I found that writing by hand not only helped me remember better, but it also helped with my English. I mainly used my laptop for recipes as I cooked for myself often. That and for doing group projects. Google Docs was also a lifesaver.

This was my first real English class after the ESL program and I was a bit intimidated. I did fine in physics and math class last term, even though it was taught in

English. Some reason I could understand scientific vernacular. It was something I was curious about too— what in my past made that easier for me? Who was I?

It was a question that popped up more frequently than not, but I tried to move on. It didn't mean I'd given up looking for answers. I just needed to have some education —to understand the world I was in before I set out on this adventure to find myself.

The professor walked in—a woman probably in her mid-thirties wearing a floral dress with knitted stockings and a long, knitted jacket. Her hair was in a messy bun and her brown eyes were hidden behind thick red-rimmed glasses. She looked like a typical hipster as one might find walking around downtown.

"All right class," she began as she logged into the computer at the front of the room. "Welcome to Writing 121. We will be working on English composition and we'll be writing many stories. To be clear, if you write anything that isn't literature, like adventures with fairies and elves or aliens, I will give you an 'F'. Genre writing is not real writing, have I made myself clear?"

No one said anything as her declaration had stunned everyone. Was this what English majors dealt with? What made sci-fi and fantasy different when it came to writing? It was stupid. I loved sci-fi, especially Doctor Who.

Something about space and time traveling excited me. It felt almost real to me—more real than what I dealt with daily. Dr. Mandy said it had to do with me not remembering my past—so everything seemed unreal to me, or that I grew up watching sci-fi. Either way, I disagreed. I thought there was more to it than that. I had done research on aliens and space travel, but all of it concluded at a dead end. The technology of this world was not advanced enough.

After writing class I had an hour for lunch. As I hadn't prepared my lunches for the week yet, I grabbed some soup from the food court. The hour gave me time to work a little on my writing homework and research new dinner recipes.

The next class, Stars and Stellar Formation, which I hoped would be a lot of fun. It was the class I looked forward to the most and hoped that it would prove to be an enjoyable class. I headed to class a bit early, excited to grab a good seat. I pulled out my notebook and textbook for the class, along with my trusty calculator. It was a TI-89 that was given to me by the parents of one student I tutored. An older sibling was getting rid of it and so she gave it to me. I was very thankful as it helped with calculus classes.

I counted 24 people in the class who all were waiting

for the class to start. I didn't see any of the same students from my writing class, which made sense. There were so many students on campus and there would be a low chance of running into anyone again.

The professor walked in, his frizzy gray hair floating around and his glasses looking as if they were an inch thick. He looked like the stereotypical professor from a TV show. I watched as he ruffled his hair and booted the class computer.

"This class is Stars and Stellar Formation. It is a 100-level class, but don't assume it will be a breeze. It will take some studying, so if you are just trying to take a class for an easy 'A', you should consider dropping it. I won't have students coming to my office the last week of class complaining that student advising said this class would help their GPA. Any questions?"

I heard a few murmurs. A student next to me got online and dropped the class right then and there. She probably stayed around only because she didn't want the professor to say anything. I figured the professor just wanted to scare the students, it couldn't be that bad.

At least, I hoped.

He began the class with details of star systems such as ours. Binary stars got a little more complicated. He went through the details of how so many stars had to have evolved and gone supernova for the right elements to form. That's the reason it took ten billion years before a solar system could have the ingredients to sustain life. He didn't think life outside of our solar system existed, but I disagreed. I believed life existed outside our solar system, the problem was that no one had found it yet. There was no doubt in my mind, though, life had to exist out there, beyond this simple planet.

I liked this class a lot more already.

Dr. Moph then went through different scenarios that could have created a habitable planet in our solar system: supernova debris, the point where gas giants formed, bombarded by large chunks of debris—how we gained our moon. All of it seemed familiar to me, as if someone had explained it before.

After he droned on for a while about different stages of the process, Dr. Moph started writing equations on the board for dust grain growth in a proto-planetary disk. I tried to stay up to speed as I scribbled them all down, along with the variable definitions. He wrote them quickly and students panicked as he erased some off the board to make room for even more terms. I wasn't too worried; the textbooks would include the equations. Hopefully.

Keeping with his fast pace, he wrote more and more

equations on the board. I did my best to keep up and as I wrote them down, I noticed something off. 7/32; it should have been 9/32.

As I stared at them, it ate at me. I knew I should say something; it could show up on a test and I didn't want everyone to get it wrong. I doubted he would show mercy on the test, even if he had given the wrong information so I raised my hand.

"Yes?" Dr. Moph rubbed the back of his neck.

"I think you meant to write 9/32 not 7/32," I glanced around. People stared at me. I shifted in my seat.

"You think?" Dr. Moph clenched his teeth.

"Actually, she's right. Says it right here." The man three seats to my left held up his tablet, his German accent apparent.

My jaw almost dropped. It was the blond man I had seen on my way to class, the one I thought I recognized. He leaned back, as if satisfied to have proven the professor wrong. The rest of the class looked at me as if I committed a cardinal sin. They shook their heads at me, frowning. At least I had one person on my side. I spun away from him, blushing.

Dr. Moph tapped his finger on the table in front of the room as he stared at the man. "What's your name?"

"Emmerich, sir."

A jolt of pain went through my skull. I had thought the migraine had passed. I pinched the bridge of my nose, an old trick to get rid of the headache. Rick. I called him Rick. But when? And where?

Dr. Moph checked the roster. "I don't see your name here."

"I'm auditing the class to see if I want to add the class to my schedule," Emmerich gave a bemused smile.

Dr. Moph studied him, squinting. "Have you taken one of my classes before?"

Emmerich shrugged. "No, I just have one of those faces."

I bit my lip. No, that wasn't it; I must have known him from before. Maybe I was closer to figuring out my past. I couldn't wait until class was over so I could to talk to him. I did not know what I would say, but I had to do something. I couldn't give up on this chance to get some answers.

Dr. Moph went back to teaching about star formation, and every so often he'd glance over, glaring, making sure I had no more comments. Great, I was already on his bad side and it was only the first day of class.

Emmerich didn't even look my way but kept his eyes on the professor, taking notes with his tablet. His tablet looked at least five years old. He must have acquired it when he was in high school. Realizing my thoughts were lingering on him and not the material Dr. Moph was giving, I quickly turned back to the board and wrote down the new set of notes just before they were erased. I did not pay tuition to get distracted in this class.

Class finished, and I turned to find Emmerich had already left. I was crestfallen. I hoped he would come to the next class so I could talk to him. At least now I had his first name. I hurried out of the class before Dr. Moph noticed. I didn't want him to say anything about correcting his equation. I was just trying to help.

With my hopes crushed and nothing else to do on campus, I started back to my apartment. I lived in a very, very small studio in Regency Apartments downtown. The doctors wanted me somewhat close to OHSU, Oregon Health and Science University, and Dr. Mandy had an office near there. I could get back using MAX's yellow line. I found riding the MAX gave me time to read, either for school or pleasure.

I didn't have much money, just a little from the government, and from scholarships and loans that helped me pay for housing. The cheapest room I could find was a studio, which was fine by me, anything was better than the hospital. I also made some money from tutoring, but I saved most of that for getting out of this town.

As I walked across campus toward the MAX station, about half a mile away, an eerie feeling swept over me. It felt like someone was watching me. Although I had run into some strange people in Portland, having to run into a store to get away from them, I found this to be different. This felt like I was being watched from afar.

Slowly, I inspected my surroundings. Students went by, ignoring me as I stood in the middle of the sidewalk. They had places to go, and I was just another obstacle to them—part of the background. As it began to rain, I glanced around, watching as people walked by, most without umbrellas as if using an umbrella was a sign of weakness. I opened mine as I stood there, causing many to dodge it as they hurried past me. It took some time but I spotted them.

Something inside me knew it was them: two men standing outside Coffeehouse-Five and staring right at me. I moved out of the middle of the path and hurried off in a different direction, my fight-or-flight reflex kicking in, but not before I got a good look at them. Both were dressed head-to-toe in black. The one on the left was tall and blond with a large scar on his right cheek and stubble covering his chin and jaw. The other had brown hair and was clean shaven with a large forehead and muscles so thick I could see them through his jacket. I immediately dubbed them "Scarface" and "Muscleman." Both looked like something out of a James Bond movie.

That was also why I chose flight over fight.

I kept on walking, checking over my shoulder until I got on the MAX. They didn't seem to follow after I noticed them, so maybe it was all in my head. I sighed as I took a seat and I opened up the book I was currently reading, Dead Moon by Peter Clines. It was about zombies on the moon, which was just cool.

I pondered whether I should tell Detective Johnson or not. He had told me to call him if anything ever came up and gave me his personal phone number. He called to check up on me occasionally, but so far, I never had a reason to call him. Yet.

The MAX stopped at the platform closest to my apartment. I grabbed my bag and got off with many of the other passengers. It was still a couple blocks to my apartment, so I opened my umbrella and hurried down the street.

It excited me to start a new term of school. Learning helped me feel like I could belong again—like a normal human. I entered the apartment complex and grabbed the keys out of my bag. I started to unlock my door when I heard a voice behind me.

"Hello Dearie, how was your first day of school?"

I jumped, still nervous that someone was following me. I turned around to find my neighbor standing in her doorway stroking her cat, Fuzzy Boots, with her TV blaring in the background. *Wheel of Fortune* was on.

"Oh, hi Ms. Collins. It went well."

She smiled, most of her teeth missing. She must have forgotten to put her dentures in today. "That's great Dearie, now don't go partying all night with all the other students in this building, you are too good for that sort of stuff."

"I won't."

She nodded and went back to watching her show. Although she could barely hear if someone was knocking on her door or when her phone rang, she always seemed to hear me when I was in the hallway.

Opening my door, I threw my backpack down and collapsed on my bed. That and my desk were the only pieces of furniture I had—or that would fit. My little apartment also had a fridge, microwave, and a tiny bathroom that they somehow fit a shower, toilet, and sink into. There were a few posters taped to the wall—one a map of the world and the others of the universe. The map of the world had 'x's all over it, representing places I had searched for any record of myself. It was weird having to research myself and find nothing. I had found other people with the same name, but none of them were me. I must not have been that interesting.

I knew I should crack open a textbook, but I really didn't feel like it. I needed to go tutor a high school student at the Lloyd Center Mall in about two hours, so I didn't want to start anything new.

When I first started out, Dr. Mandy asked if I would tutor her high school daughter in math and science. She was so impressed that she told other parents and now I made money doing this. It wasn't something I loved doing, but it passed the time and helped me save up to leave after I got my GED and Associates Degrees. I didn't know where I would start, but it would be somewhere warmer than Portland.

I glanced at the clock on the oven. Ten to four. I let out a deep breath and bit my lip, thinking of what I could do for the rest of the afternoon. I had to tutor at six. That left me enough time to watch an episode of Grimm before heading out.

My stomach grumbled. All I had were some grapes and crackers to snack on. I glanced at the time again. It was still too early for dinner, but I would need something to hold me over until after the tutor session, and grapes and crackers just would not cut it. No, I wanted something sweet.

I jumped up from my bed. I needed a Voodoo Donut. Grabbing my purse, I hurried out the door and onto the street.

Nothing made me happier than one of those strange donuts. They had every flavor, from maple bacon to bubble gum—they even had a Neapolitan donut. It wasn't too far from my apartment complex, and from there I could catch the MAX to Lloyd Center where I was to meet Pete, the high school student I tutored on Mondays. Today was also the first day of school, so I felt could treat myself.

It was still drizzling outside, the rain somehow still hitting my face even with my umbrella. I didn't understand how that was possible, but apparently it was. I decided that the umbrella was worthless and put it away, just relying on my hoodie I had purchased from a thrift store. It was just a normal black hoodie with cool galaxy art on it. It was one of my favorites and it was becoming well worn.

I started humming. No song in particular, just random notes that popped into my head. I could never remember the melody of any specific song, so I always bunched them together and made my own music. It probably sounded horrible to any passerby but to me it made me feel content.

A car honked as I nearly stepped out in front of it. The light was green for me, not them. I waved anyway as they drove off. Rolling my eyes, I returned to my music. This time I think I started humming "Not the Villain" by S.J. Tucker.

True names, stopped clocks, wildest dreams
Time's up, darling; let it be

I loved walking in the city and watching as other Portlanders went by. Portland encompassed such diversity: from students to hipsters, to Chinese and Scandinavians. It felt like I was getting a taste of what the rest of the world was like.

I glanced over to find a Wesen, from the TV show Grimm, on a park bench. At least, he looked like a Wesen —his hair wiry and long, face scruffy, and his eyes even madder than a hatter. Not that Wesen existed, but I still had a fear of them. Wesen were creatures that appeared human but once they were stressed or attacked, or you had Grimm blood in you, you could see the creature inside. Since being in Portland, I had watched a few shows that were filmed in the city, *Grimm* being one of them. Now I was always looking over my shoulder, making sure no weird creature was about to attack. I hurried away from the man sitting on the bench. You could never be too careful.

As for the show Portlandia, I found that every person I met fit into one episode or another. I've watched people ask their waitress where their chicken was from, seen people play hide-and-seek in libraries, and don't get me started on putting a bird on things. There were birds everywhere in Portland— you would think this city was an aviary. I thought the show was a documentary until someone told me otherwise. I still believed they were wrong.

A young man with a green mohawk walked by, his leather jacket studded with silver spikes and his baggy jeans hanging off his hips. Young stubble covered some of his acne scars and a cut ran down the side of his cheek. He pointed ahead, showing something to his friend, tattoos on his knuckles spelling out 'REBL' in black ink. The girl nodded, running her fingers through her short blue hair. Her clothes were similar; a leather jacket and jeans. She giggled, her piercings looking as if they would split her lip as her mouth opened. I never understood lip rings—they seemed like they would always get in the way, not to mention hurt like hell.

The girl grabbed him by the arm and pulled him down the street. He pulled her close and kissed her. How did he not cut his lip on that piercing? She glanced over, seeing that I was staring.

"Take a picture, it lasts longer!" she yelled and flipped me off.

Peering down, I hurried off in the direction I needed to go. I hated when I did that, my mind carrying me off in a different world and found myself staring at someone. I felt like such an idiot.

After I got out of their sight, I stretched my arms and thought about the couple again. At least they had each other. I wished I could find someone like that, someone I connected with. I had acquaintances, sure, but most of them were just classmates. I got to talk about gossip with some of them, but that was about it. I had no true friends. No one to stay up all night just talking. No one to hold my hand as I stumbled through my life.

Although this city wasn't bad, it just didn't feel like home. I had gone through picture after picture of different cities, none of them triggering any memory. There were still a lot of places I needed to search, but it still worried me. Would I never remember my home? Was I destined to never go back? I wouldn't give up trying though. Maybe I would start searching in Arizona next. I heard it never rains there.

The screeching wheels of a railcar made me jump about five feet into the air. That sound got me every time. I swore they should have warning signs: "Danger, high pitch screeching. Mind your ears," just like London had "Mind the Gap." But nevertheless, there were no sign and I would forever hurt my ears.

I glanced over at the trolley as it came to a halt. Passengers got on and off to be carried across town. I always preferred walking but if I had to travel far, I took the MAX.

I turned down Burnside. I was almost there, my mouth watering with anticipation, even though I knew that the line would be long, and it would take another ten minutes before I got my donut. At least I could breathe in the sugary air that emanated from the store.

As I walked down the street, three men were coming straight at me. I felt my hands shake. They weren't the same men I had seen at Subway but fear spread throughout my body. All three of them wore the same dark clothing as the others. But unlike them, these three wore sunglasses. I couldn't tell if they were looking at me.

Although they were mixed in a crowd, they stood out like a sore thumb. They all stood tall and military-like, almost as if they were henchmen in a James Bond movie. That was what caught my eye—they had the same demeanor as the others. Two of them had black hair and high cheekbones indicating they could be related. The third was larger and had a beard. Their coats had a bulge on the side, revealing that they had some gun holstered underneath. I gulped.

As they moved in, I tried to stay clear of them. Maybe if I hurried by, they wouldn't notice me. Maybe they weren't even looking for me, maybe they were part of some secret mission to take down some Wesen. Yes, I would keep telling myself that.

Then why did I have a feeling that I had been in this situation before?

I rushed past The Brothers and Beardy. They didn't stop walking forward or turn to see where I was going. I took a deep breath and released it slowly. Imagination was getting the better of me, maybe I should stop watching sci-fi.

Like that would ever happen.

I didn't see the men again. I needed to stop freaking myself out, and a donut would be the perfect cure.

I got in line behind an elderly woman with her two grandsons and waited. Good thing I still had an hour and a half before I had to tutor.

"Hey Angela."

I turned to find Detective Johnson in line right behind me, his suit and tie looking as straight as ever. His brown hair was cut close to his head, and I had never seen his face anything but clean shaven. Detective Lang, his partner, was right beside him, her blonde hair pulled back in a bun and her lady suit as crisp as Johnson's.

I greeted him with a hug. "Detective Johnson!" I turned to his partner. I didn't dare hug her, I learned my lesson the first time. "Detective Lang! It's great to see you both!"

"Likewise." He straightened his tie. "Didn't you just have your first day of the new term? How was that?"

The detectives had helped me out a lot since the accident. Both were called to the scene and assigned to my case when I was found. I learned that Detective Johnson had a daughter about my age, which explained why he wanted to assist on my case so much. I don't think he could imagine his own daughter going through the same things I was going through.

"It was great, other than correcting the professor on an equation. Pretty sure he hates me now."

Detective Johnson let out a deep laugh. "Now that's funny. It's great that you are doing so well."

"And I wouldn't worry about the professor, you will like some and hate others," Detective Lang added. "Is everything else going okay?"

I debated telling them about the men I had seen that day. There wasn't anything they could do, but I knew I would regret it if I didn't. And they would be really pissed if they found out later. I scratched my arm. "I sorta feel like I'm being followed. I'm not sure why. There are two men in black that I keep running into that make me feel nervous. I don't know if it's my imagination..."

He furrowed his eyebrows. "Have they done anything to make you feel like they want to hurt you?"

I shook my head. "No, I don't know if they were looking at me or something behind me. I'm probably imagining things."

"Don't let your guard down, Angela. If you see anything that seems suspicious, let us know right away," Detective Lang added.

Detective Johnson pulled out a card. "I will have some of our men keep an eye out around your apartment for the next week. I know you already have my card, but here is another in case you lost it. If you notice them again, don't be afraid to call."

Taking the card, I thanked both for their help. "Do you have any new leads?"

Detective Lang answered. "Regretfully, no. We have found nothing. But keep your chin up, we'll find something, eventually."

I tried to smile but my heart ached inside. They'd been saying that for the past year and still they had found nothing. How was that even possible? How was it possible to not find someone in this day and age of technology?

The line shifted, and we made it into the little shop at last. Rows and rows of donuts filled the racks. It always astounded me how many types of donuts they offered. Some people took forever to pick out what they wanted, but I had come for one particular donut and I would not settle for anything less. I went up on my tiptoes to check the front. Pink scribbles on the chalkboard told me my favorite, the Captain My Captain, a donut with vanilla frosting and Captain Crunch on top, was still available. I could feel the diabetes coming for me.

Detective Johnson pulled out his wallet. "Which one do you want?"

I blushed. "No, it's fine, you need not buy me a donut."

"Please, it's my treat. Just pick one. I'm already getting a couple dozen for a quick celebration at work. It's no problem."

I told the man at the register what I wanted, and Detective Johnson paid for it. I hated it when people bought me things, it was embarrassing. After other customers shoved us back out onto the street, I thanked him for everything again.

"Remember to call me if you need anything," he said

as he and Detective Lang waved as they went off in the other direction. I hoped I wouldn't need to.

I headed toward the MAX and took a deep whiff of the sugary goodness that was the Captain, My Captain donut. I chomped down on it, the Captain Crunch topping spilling everywhere. I should have been more careful. I kicked the pieces off the sidewalk and crossed the street, ignoring the grumpy old lady that frowned at me for littering. It wasn't my fault they didn't provide enough napkins, and besides, it was biodegradable.

A few minutes went by before the MAX approached, making its beeping and screeching sound as it entered the station. I waited for passengers to get off before I jumped in and wrapped my arm around one of the poles. I needed both hands for my donut which I tried to savor by taking small bird-like bites. It was probably why I was making such a big mess.

As more people gathered on the train, I caught sight of the three men; The Brothers and Beardy. They stood across the street, staring at me as I rode off toward Lloyd Center. I thought about getting out the card Detective Johnson gave me and calling him, but I realized I had no way to do that. I had left the cell phone in my backpack and didn't have it on me.

Coincidentally, I had an intensely strange feeling come

over me, a feeling that everything would change. Whether it would be for the better or for the worse, I didn't know. I just felt like something would change. I savored the last bite of my donut. There was no point in worrying about it now, I had a student to tutor.

I arrived at Lloyd Center ten minutes before I was to meet with my student, Pete. He was a tenth grader who required help with Chemistry and Algebra II. He was a smart kid, he just needed to learn to focus on his schoolwork and not spend his time playing video games or on Facebook. I had a feeling that he tried to do his work on time only to impress me, which I didn't mind. At least he was getting it done.

Although I didn't have enough time to go shopping, I had enough time to get a seat and watch some ice skating. That was the one great things about Lloyd Center, it had an all-year round ice rink in the middle of the mall. Unless a parent wanted me to meet here, I didn't get to come to this mall often. I was practically broke after I paid for rent and food, and adding to my savings, and didn't have much money to spend on stuff I didn't need.

I found a place to sit and waited for Pete. We met here since his sister took ice skating lessons at the same time I tutored him. She was cute to watch, too, as she had just started elementary school this last year. They would practice routines for different holidays to show the parents what they were learning, even though most of the parents watched them during practice. It was the thought that counted.

Their mother was glad that I could meet at the same time, that way she didn't have to make two trips for her children, and I was glad to do that for her. Pete said she was scary when she didn't get her way, so I was glad to be on her good side.

I tapped my finger to the beats of the song that played: "Somebody I Used to Know" by Gotye. I hadn't heard it in a while, surprisingly. A few months ago, the mall had it playing all the time, along with some other rock songs I didn't care for. After the song ended, one of those song I didn't care for began. "Umbrella" by Rihanna. It wasn't like I hated it, but it seemed like Portland radio stations had it playing on the radio anytime it rained, which was often.

Dang it. Now that tune would be stuck in my head the rest of the night.

"Hi Miss Starr," Pete, greeted. His light brown hair was shaggy and messed up, covering his light hazel eyes. He set his books down on the table. I watched as his sister put on her hot pink skates and followed her friends onto the rink. Their mom took a seat a few tables away and pulled out her computer. I believed she was an event coordinator, but I could have been mistaken. Maybe it was architecture.

I straightened up in my chair. "Hello Pete. How was your first day back at school?"

He beamed. "My teacher asked me a question in class and I got it right."

"That's great! Soon you won't need my help at all."

He blushed and opened up his notebook. "Wasn't today your first day as well? College must be so cool."

"It's all right. Lots of studying so you better get into a good habit now before you start college." I smiled to myself.

He nodded, and we spent the next hour going over homework for chemistry and math.

With a bag of Chinese food in hand, I headed back toward my apartment. As my stomach was growling by the time the tutoring session was over, I treated myself with the cash Pete's mom had given me. I had a craving for lemon chicken and August Moon had the best Chinese food in town. I had tried other restaurants, but it never tasted nearly as good.

Shadows scurried across the pavement, as if in a hurry to greet the darkness. With every step I took more and more shadows seemed to appear. My once happy mood was dwindling. I felt as if the shadows were surrounding me, getting ready to attack. The darkness seemed familiar, and it was suffocating. It felt like long tendrils that were wrapping around me. I clutched my bag of food and walked even faster. My heart felt like it would jump out of my chest. My mouth felt dry, and I felt like my mind was in a box, unable to recognize what was real and what was in my head. The doctors said since they had found me in the middle of the night, more than likely the fear had to do with whatever it was I had experienced. I believed there was something more to it than that.

What had happened to me that made me feel like this—to fear such little things?

The clattering of tree branches did not help my nerves. I studied everyone to make sure they weren't part of the group of men I saw earlier. None were.

A black cat ran right in front of me, hissing as I nearly stepped on its tail. It slashed at my leg and then scurried away into the darkness. I nearly screamed. Stupid cat, it almost gave me a heart attack. Wasn't it bad luck when a black cat crossed your path? I thought I saw a little white on its chest. Yeah, I would keep telling myself that.

I could see my apartment now and my muscles began to relax. I was safe now—just a few more steps. I had escaped my fear and I could eat my Chinese in peace, with no cats hissing at me.

Escape. The word resonated with me. Something felt as if it was pushing against my mind. I remembered a hand trying to grab me, but I had shoved the person away. Darkness covered his face, but I could hear his laughter— deep and frightening. Had I been escaping something when they found me?

A wave of pain shot through my head. Not again. My knees betrayed me and I almost fell to the ground. Luckily, I was standing near a railing and grabbed it before I could fall. The food didn't drop, thank goodness. My stomach would have killed me if I had spilt it all.

After a moment, I shook off the feeling and pulled my keys out of my pocket. It was the third time today something like this had happened. Could it just be a coincidence? Or was something happening so that I would get some answers?

I unlocked the door to find my apartment was how I left it: bare and incomplete. It looked rather sad and empty. But a few weeks ago, I had caved, and got a real bed. I was tired of sleeping on a cot.

I set the food down on the kitchen counter and opened the window. I needed fresh air without having to step outside again, even if it was still raining and cold. I didn't want a repeat of what had just happened, and I didn't want that black cat to come back and claw me again. All I needed was to have to go to the doctor for some stitches or a rabies shot.

I took in a deep breath of the wet pavement smell. I was thankful this window worked, as I heard other tenants complain that theirs got stuck all the time.

As I looked down at the street, I saw something out of the corner of my eye. At a second glance, there was nothing there. I looked around again, but nothing seemed out of place. I swore I saw something moving around. Maybe it was that cat again. I loved cats, but that black cat from earlier scared me.

I scanned around once more. It probably was nothing, just my imagination. Detective Johnson said they would have their men check around occasionally, so I was safe. I could trust them, I knew, so I didn't let it bother me anymore. I checked the locks on my door one more time, grabbed a fork and dug into my lemon chicken. The song "Umbrella" was still stuck in my head. Stupid repetitive lyrics and catchy tune.

Beep. Beep. Beep.

I slammed my hand on my alarm clock. Was it morning already? I checked the time. 6:30. I rubbed my face with my palm. Ugh. I hated mornings.

Reluctantly, I pulled myself out of bed and started the water for the shower. I had an hour to get ready for history, which unfortunately started at eight-thirty in the morning. It was like they wanted you to fail. I was definitely a night person, preferring to stay up late and stare at the stars. In the future, I would have to find a job where I could just stay up at night and not deal with mornings. Mornings wouldn't even exist in my book. I had a feeling I would be a lot happier.

However, at least for the time being, I would have to endure early mornings. With English as a second language, I could take mostly night classes, which was great, but since I was moving forward from that program, I had to take regular classes, which were usually in the morning. At least it made scheduling tutoring a lot easier.

After drying my hair, putting on some fresh clothes and light makeup, I went in search of some breakfast. I needed to make a stop at a grocery store today as I was out of most everything. Luckily, there was a café in Portland for every citizen, I swore. I doubted any city had this many, except maybe somewhere in France. I wouldn't know from experience; it's just seemed like every picture of Paris had a café in it.

Grabbed a cup of English Breakfast and a cheese

Danish from Food For Thought Café, I headed toward the MAX. I had left my books at home after Pete let me know that his older brother only took them to class if the professor said to. This made my backpack super light, and I was very thankful for that.

The best thing about getting breakfast at a café was having the warm food and drink feel as if it was heating me up from the inside out. The cold really got to me as I spent a lot more time outside than last year because I had to travel to the college. I hated how cold it was getting and a lot of people were saying they expected heavy snow this month. Although snow was beautiful, I didn't want to see how disastrous travel around the city would become. I had heard horror stories.

I sipped some tea and nearly spit it out. It was hot, really, really hot. I swallowed it but not before burning my tongue and my throat. Why did cafés always do that? Did they want people to burn themselves on their tea? It was stupid as it always took over an hour for the tea to cool down. The next time I bought tea, I was going to ask for some ice cubes and not care if they gave me weird looks. I could see it now, "Do you want an iced tea?" "No, I just want a tea that doesn't burn the epidermis off of my tongue."

After I grabbed a seat on the MAX, I took a bite of my

cheese Danish. It was one of my favorite breakfast pastries, the creamy center complimented the fluffy bread that surrounded it. I grinned as I took another bite. So yummy. Luckily, I could still taste it after that tea.

Arriving to the station next to campus, I hoped the professor wouldn't mind me drinking tea. I heard some professors didn't want any food or drink in their classroom, which never made sense to me. We are humans, we need substance! If they thought it was distracting, I think it is more distracting to be hungry and only thinking about what to eat once class was over. Not to mention my stomach grumbled louder than any other person and people would stare at me. No, eating and drinking in classrooms should be permitted.

The classroom was small, only a handful of chairs and desks. I took a chair near the front, hoping it would help me understand the lessons better, especially when I was still trying to understand the history of this world. It felt all so new to me.

A few other students were already in their seats waiting for the class to start. I wasn't the greatest at starting a conversation with a stranger, as I didn't quite know what to talk about. I always had a fear they would find out about my history and ask questions, or feel pity for me. So, I kept to myself and tried not to get in anyone's way.

A nearly 6-foot-tall girl about the same age as me walked in. She looked like a model from a gothic magazine with her long hair dyed a dark purple and so many piercings that I lost count. She definitely stood out, but she also was strikingly beautiful. She walked over to near where I was sitting.

"Is this seat taken?" she asked.

I shook my head. "Oh, no it isn't."

"Thanks." She set her things down and took a seat. I tried not to stare at her as she moved a piece of her purple hair behind her ear that had two industrial bar piercings. She glanced over at me through the corner of her eye. I looked away quickly, trying not to appear like the idiot I was. She giggled a little.

"I'm used to people staring at me, don't worry about it."

I blushed. I didn't mean to stare and now I felt like I was being rude. "Sorry, I didn't mean to, I just thought your piercings and hair were really pretty."

"Oh, thanks. I like to switch up the colors for fun. Keeps life entertaining, especially if you are stuck somewhere and want to do something to feel a little freer."

I thought she had a good point. Changing outward appearances, clothes, hair, and so on was a good way to escape. It helped show that you didn't want to submit to the world around you, but to stand out and be yourself. I hoped we would get to know each other more throughout the term, but I was too shy to talk to her more now.

The professor stepped in and interrupted my thoughts, which wasn't a terrible thing. Dr. McKenzie looked excited, the opposite of Dr. Moph, with his crimson hair quickly spiked and his eyes bright and enthusiastic. Personally, I couldn't believe anyone would be happy this early in the morning. He introduced himself and plugged his USB into the computer. He looked a little young to be a professor, especially compared to the astronomy professor. Once all the data was transferred from his stick-drive, he started class.

We did a general overview of what Dr. McKenzie would expect from us for the term. There wasn't much he expected, other than for us to show up to class and do our homework. It seemed odd that a lot of professors had to say that, as if students weren't doing the two things that should be a normal thing. I never understood why people skipped classes since they were paying for them.

After history class I had meditation. The college required I take a P.E. class, and I felt meditation would help me calm and center myself. I was supposed to be doing it anyway, as Dr. Mandy told me to meditate daily for thirty minutes, but I was bad at remembering it. At least this way I did each week during class. All I had to do was show up to pass.

I felt much better after meditation. The instructor was very kind, helping people de-stress and focus on the task at hand. I wished we had this class every day, as it would help me get through the day. There were clubs for meditation, but they were very early in the morning and I didn't want to come all the way to school at seven.

I had two hours before I had calculus class after which I would have to head home. Tonight, I was to tutor a student at Powell's Bookstore and needed to get groceries. I decided I would head to the library and crack open one of the calculus textbooks they had available to get an idea of what we would cover today. Then, if I had time, I could get a head start on some astronomy homework, although there wasn't too much homework in that class yet.

The PCC Cascade Library was rather cool looking. One side of it was rounded with glass that looked out over the lawn. In the fall it was nice, as the leaves of the trees were changing color and I loved to sit at the windows and stare out at the beauty of it all.

As I walked in, I savored the powerful scent of books. I loved books of every type; fiction and nonfiction, fantasy, poetry, biology, history. Learning was a hobby for me, it was the first thing I did to recover my memory, but no story ever seemed familiar to me.

I passed through the rows of shelves and past the reception desk. Mrs. Jennings waved at me from behind the reference desk and I waved back. Yeah, I spent way too much time here already, and it was only my first day of school. I passed by her and started up the stairs.

Heading up to the second floor, I found a place next to the windows so I could look outside as I read. Even though it wasn't that nice of a day, I still enjoyed sitting near natural light rather than hide away in some corner with shelves.

Grabbing a table near the windows, I pulled out my notebook and wrote my name and the date on the top of the page. I tapped my pencil next to the date I wrote. January 7th. Had it really been exactly one year since my accident? My fingers grasped for my necklace. Was that why I felt so weird this week?

At least they said it was an accident. The doctors thought someone had thrown me out of a car near Portland's Chinatown. Someone found me passed out on the street with cuts and bruises all over my body. They called the police and took me to the hospital. My first memory was waking up in OHSU and seeing strange men in white gowns hovering over me. It was the scariest experience ever. I had a few broken ribs, lacerations on my arms and legs, and a giant bruise on my forehead. They asked me who I was, and I couldn't answer them. They asked me where I was from and I still couldn't answer them. When they found me, I was wearing a necklace with the name Angela Starr etched on it. That was all they had to work with.

That might not even be my real name. It was the name written on the necklace I had but it could have been anything. Was it someone else's name? Was it the designer's trademark? I had no idea, but it felt right to be called Angela. So, I kept it.

Focusing back on my homework, I started the first problem: calculations using the new equations Dr. Moph had given us. Hopefully he had used the correct one this time, but I some reason doubted it.

I scribbled on my to-do list, checking off that piece of homework. With a smirk of satisfaction, I went to the next item: calculus. I shuffled through my purple notebook, grabbed the library textbook, and started to read. The first chapter was mainly a review of what we covered last term, which was a great refresher.

I leaned back in my chair and checked the time. It wasn't even noon yet, which gave me a chance to grab a bite to eat before calculus class. I wondered if every homework assignment would be this simple. Probably not.

Twirling the pencil between my fingers, I debated what I would do after I got my GED. I knew I wanted to travel, but I debated if I would want to further my studies and earn a degree. I enjoyed astronomy and could see myself doing that, but considering how much time classes were taking me to get my GED, I felt that a college degree would put my goal to find out who I was on hold. So, I had no idea what I should do after this year. There was time to figure it out, but I wanted to plan it all out now. Dr. Mandy said it would be best to take a year off to explore and then decide. It had already been a year since everything had happened so only taking a year off seemed like it wouldn't be enough time. I felt like I was even further from the truth. So, what was I supposed to do?

I glanced around the library and saw students cruising by, exploring their future, making new friends... and here I was with no idea where I was going. I liked astronomy and space, but what did I want to do with that? Did I want to become a professor? Research? But research what? There were so many possibilities, it was overwhelming.

Funny, for all the things I knew, why couldn't I know

myself?

As I stared outside, two figures caught my eye. Two men in black were staring up at the library windows. Scarface and Muscleman. Were they watching me? I shuddered. They were looking up here, maybe it was just a coincidence. Just like the day before. I shook my head. No, one thing I had learned from *Doctor Who* was that there were no such things as coincidences.

I gathered my things and hurried toward the back exit. I could lose them by going out that way. They probably had no idea about that exit and I could sneak to my next class.

My pace quickened, and I crashed through the door open to the outside. Not paying attention to what was in front of me for fear of what was behind me, I ran straight into something.

I fell, my butt hitting the concrete with a loud thud. My backpack took most of the impact and I flailed on my back like a turtle. A really stupid turtle.

"I'm so sorry. Are you all right?"

Oh crap, please don't be who I think it is. I looked up to find Emmerich kneeling beside me. I blushed. Why did I have to be so clumsy in front of him? But at least now I could talk to him.

"I'm fine, I'm good. Don't worry about it," I mumbled

as he helped me up. His look of concern made me feel all warm inside. What was this feeling? Why did seeing him always make my heart quicken? I had just met the man.

"Are you sure? I can take you to a doctor..."

I shook my head. "No, I'm okay. Really."

We stood there in awkward silence. I straightened the straps of the backpack.

"Sorry, how rude of me." He held out his hand and smiled, dimples appearing on his cheeks making him look younger than he was. "I'm Emmerich."

Taking his hand, I nodded. "Yeah, I'm Angela. Thanks for backing me up yesterday with Dr. Moph."

He laughed. "That's right, I thought you looked familiar."

Oh, so he didn't recognize me, even from class, let alone from before the accident. A blow straight to my ego. "So, are you going to join the class?" My heart raced with hope of a yes.

He grinned. "I think I just might."

I blushed again and tried to change the subject. "So, where are you headed?"

"Inside the library. I've got a bunch of research to do already."

Damn, wrong way. Didn't matter, I had class soon anyway. I debated asking if he wanted to get a bite to eat before his work, but he already clarified that he was too busy. "Oh, that sucks."

He shrugged. "Work comes with school, what can I say?"

"Which class is it for? I might add it to my schedule. I was thinking about adding another class." The moment that comment came out of my mouth, I wished I could take it back. I sounded desperate, like a stalker. I wasn't a stalker, at least I didn't think I was. Just curious.

Curious about this hot stranger. Not stalker material at all.

He scratched his head. "It's individual research for a professor."

"That sounds interesting, which professor?"

"Um," he glanced down at his watch. "For Dr. Creekman."

It was clear he needed to get to work. Too bad, I really wanted to talk to him some more. "Well then, I guess I will see you around?"

"You can count on it." He turned and went back toward the library. I could feel my cheeks turn even redder. Curse my fair skin.

Suddenly I remembered why I had been leaving the library in such haste. I looked around, but there was no sign of the two men. Filled with relief, I headed straight to calculus class.

Calculus class was what I expected—we mainly reviewed what we had gone over in the last class. I was excited for Thursday when we would start doing vectors. It was new to me and I enjoyed learning how the universe worked.

After class I headed toward the MAX. I would swing by the grocery store to prepare something for dinner, probably soup since it was simple, and I could purchase a pressure cooker which made cooking so much easier. I could just put everything in the pressure cooker and push a button and presto, dinner.

I learned how to shop for groceries quickly instead of taking forever to pick out what I needed. The key was having the recipe on hand, so you knew what you needed at that moment and didn't have to peruse and figure it out as you went—that only led to buying a lot of snacks.

After going to the store, I headed back home to rest a little before going to tutor. I decided it would be best to prep the food for the pressure cooker so that I could start it the moment I got back. Chopping up some winter squash, onion, and garlic, I thought it would be best to keep the beans and pasta in their containers as there would be no point to opening those early. I couldn't wait to have dinner, prepping always made me hungry. Good thing I got some chocolate as a snack.

As I munched on a piece of chocolate, I glanced at the clock and figured I should head to my first tutoring session. Except for Peter, I met most of my students at Powell's Book Store. Thankfully it was no hassle for the parents and I got to pick up new books every couple of days. Grabbing a couple novels to trade in, I left my apartment.

Since it was only a fifteen-minute walk, I probably spent more time there than anywhere else in Portland. I loved to learn and reading helped with my English and to escape from my worries. So many people didn't use books as an escape, or even pick up new things to learn, and I found that to be odd. Were people content enough to just go on with their lives and not change anything about themselves or their outlook on life?

Opening my umbrella, I tried to make sure the books I was trading in stayed dry on the walk to the store. That was always my fear: that the books would get wet and they would be ruined, and I wouldn't get any money for them. Then I would have to use more of my allowance, which sucked. I knew I could always go to the library to check out books, but for a lot of the ones I wanted to read, I didn't want to get on a waitlist. And I wanted to support a local business as much as I could.

At Powell's, I exchanged my books for in-store credit and began to explore. Powell's had many floors to venture through and I couldn't decide where to start. Signs pointed every which way to different genres. Should I pick up a science fiction novel? A history novel perhaps? The choices were endless.

I went up the stairs to science fiction and fantasy. I could see the sign for the horror genre section. With everything going on, I knew that it would be a mistake to venture in there. So I stuck to science fiction. Some stories made me feel at peace, as if I could live in a place where aliens and spaceships existed. It was a fantasy of mine, to run off with the Doctor or some alien. But things like that never happened.

Browsing, I found a book called *Icarus Hunt* by Timothy Zahn. It looked interesting, so I grabbed it. It would keep me occupied for a good while. Now I just had to choose one more.

As I started through the fantasy section, I saw my first student come in. I motioned him over to a table and we began our session.

Emmerich didn't show up to class. I peered around the

room one more time but didn't see his gorgeous face. I had hoped for a friend to study with but now I was stuck by myself. Although I would always worry he would find out the truth, which wouldn't be hard to figure out I knew nothing about my past. I could lie and tell him some made-up story, but if we got serious, and he found out the truth, he wouldn't be able to trust anything else I had to say.

Dr. Moph started class. I took notes but my mind wandered. Why didn't Emmerich show up? Maybe it ended up not fitting his schedule, or maybe he just didn't want to deal with the professor's attitude. I sure didn't. Whatever the reason had been, I just hoped I would run into him again.

Class finished, and I didn't have any tutoring sessions, so I got to relax and start up a new series on Netflix. It was a toss-up between *Arrow*, *Vampire Diaries*, and *Teen Wolf*. I debated between the three the whole way back to my apartment.

I got back and stuck some soup I had made the night before in the microwave, which was the last of any food I had, and turned on my laptop. I decided to watch *Vampire Diaries* to see what this vampire fad was all about.

About four episodes into it, I figured it out. Hot, sexy bad guys.

* * *

Thursday came and went and I got the good news that one of my students had aced her first pop quiz. I felt very proud that she had increased her grade in such a short time frame. It usually took a couple of months before a student could grasp the material on their own. Even though I was happy for her, it also meant that she would leave me soon and I would have to find another student.

Now Friday was here, and all I had was my astronomy lab, which I was looking forward to. If it was anything like last term, then it would be mostly on computers doing simulations and simple math. Although I wished it were more intense, I found it to be a good intro to what astrophysics was all about. However, I felt like it was probably a lie and astrophysics was much more complicated.

The TA, Kim, was already in the lab, her short red hair making her stand out. Piercings speckled her ears and nose. Her arm had a Chinese dragon tattoo and her nails were painted a deep purple. She indicated to sign in and grab a seat at a computer. I did as she wanted and found a computer that was empty. Although we would probably be in pairs, I took an empty computer and let whoever wanted to join me to do so. I was too afraid to walk up to someone to ask to join them for them to say no, they are waiting for someone else. I always felt embarrassed when that was the case.

As I waited for the lab to start, more students wandered in, writing their name on the check-in sheet and grabbing a seat. Most people had partners, and I was still alone. I grew anxious, fiddling with my nails, hoping the TA wouldn't point out that I was alone and make someone be partners with me. I've had that happen before and it was more embarrassing than getting rejected because someone was waiting for a friend.

Just when I thought all hope was lost, a familiar face walked through the lab doors. It felt like my heart skipped a beat when Emmerich turned to me and smiled. Walking over, he signed in and took a seat next to me.

He put his backpack down. "So, you're in this lab section too?"

I nodded. "Yeah, glad to see you added it to your class. I didn't see you on Wednesday so I thought maybe you weren't able to add the class."

"I had to rearrange a class on Wednesdays that I forgot about, but I was able to figure it out with both professors."

"Sweet, I'm glad we will get to take the class together." I blushed a little, realizing what I had just said.

"Yeah, me too." He smiled. I hoped my cheeks weren't

as red as they felt.

I turned to the computer. "I guess we should switch this on and get ready."

"Yeah, probably a good idea."

Switching on the computer, I made a note of how close Emmerich was sitting next to me. He was close, but not uncomfortably close. I felt relaxed with him there and he felt almost familiar. I enjoyed being around him, as it was the first time I felt a connection and a sense of belonging.

The T.A. Kim started class and explained the activity for the day. We were all to be given different events in the universe's history and place it where it would be located if the history of all the universe happened within a year, called a cosmic calendar. This was to show how humans have existed for a little time compared to the history of the universe, and so on. It showed us how grand everything was and how we can't comprehend the universe in our human minds. We were tiny in the grand scheme of things.

Each group was to pull three events out of a basket and place them on the calendar year. The two of us got when dinosaurs roamed the Earth, the Big Bang, and the Formation of the Solar System. Between the two of us, it wasn't hard to figure out where to put them. We just transferred the year into seconds and then divided that by how many seconds there are in 13.8 billion years. From there we would get the dates.

The Big Bang, of course, was the beginning of the universe so it was January 1st. We wrote on our lab worksheet.

"Easy peasy." Emmerich smiled.

"Yeah, now we just have to figure out the other two," I said.

The two of us split the calculations and I would figure out when the solar system was created and Emmerich would figure out when dinosaurs roamed the Earth. After doing some math, I figured out when it was.

"I got it being on Dec 25th." I showed him my calculations.

"Yeah, that looks right. I got the 2nd of September for mine."

I looked over his calculations and nodded. "Yeah looks correct to me. I guess we did it, other than filling out what we learned from this assignment."

He nodded. "Yeah, which is easy—we learned that humans are insignificant when looking at the big picture, and think they are the only living beings in this vast galaxy, which is a great mistake."

I glanced up at him. "You think other intelligent beings exist?"

Emmerich smiled a little. "Without a doubt. It makes little sense that this world is the only one. I think there are many planets, not to mention the fact that there are probably different dimensions as well."

"It would be cool to travel these planets and travel everywhere, wouldn't it?"

"Yeah, I think it would. Anyway, should we turn this in?"

I nodded, and we gathered our things, logged out of the computer, and handed in our assignment. Kim checked over our work and said that we had gotten the right answers. We said our goodbyes and headed out of the lab.

"So, did I miss anything fun in class on Wednesday?" Emmerich asked as we stood outside the room.

I shook my head. "No, he went over more information about proto-planetary disks and star formation."

"Did you have to correct him again?" he laughed.

"No, fortunately."

"What? It was great that you caught that. You totally got on his nerves."

"That's exactly what I didn't want to do on the first day of class."

"Well, he deserved to be called out like that. He treats his students horribly."

"So, will you be in class on Monday?"

He nodded. "Yeah, I'll be there."

I blushed. "Well, maybe we could meet beforehand and I could get you a copy of those notes."

"I would like that. How about I meet you around one at the library where we bumped into each other?"

"Yeah, sounds good."

He waved as he headed the opposite way I was going. "See you around, Angela."

My heart was racing as I watched him leave. I felt like jumping up and down. I had made a friend at last and I wanted to shout it out to the world. I felt connected to Emmerich.

Rick.

I grabbed my head. Pain shot through it. It was worse than the one I had a few days earlier. I knelt down for a second before the pain started to fade. An image flashed through my mind. It was of Emmerich. We were sitting at a table and he was showing me a map of the solar system. His soft fingers glossed over my hand as he showed me secrets of the universe.

What was that?

Had I met Emmerich before? The pain was debilitating and I couldn't think. I needed to get to my apartment and take something for my head.

In my apartment I went straight for my herb drawer.

One hobby I picked up was herbal medicine. I hated conventional medicine, especially the pills they had given me after the accident. I told myself, never again. I had tried taking a rosemary and gingko tincture hoping to restore my lost memories. It didn't work but I felt my short-term memory was a lot clearer.

I snatched the tincture and took two dropperfuls. It was a mixture of valerian, passionflower, feverfew, and California Poppy. Valerian had to be one of the strongest tasting herbs, its taste never left your mouth. I had gotten used to it but the taste still lingered. Some people hated the taste and found that it had an opposite effect and kept them up at night, but it was pure magic for me.

I laid down on my bed, staring up at my poster of the Orion Nebula, admiring the beautiful, colorful clouds with the hundreds of stars forming inside. Scientists called it a star nursery. Things like that fascinated me, I wanted to know all the answers to the universe. That was why I took science classes, to seek the answers, even though I know I won't be able to answer them all. Truly, I just wished I could venture into space, see all these amazing things we study.

Maybe that was why I liked *Doctor Who*. Through the show, I could travel through time and space. If I were a Time Lord, I could go anywhere I wanted and at any time. Except, of course, I wouldn't be able to go back and change what I had already done. Crazy, really, how they played with the laws of time and space and yet, somehow, it all made sense. Wibbly-wobbly, timey-wimey stuff I supposed.

Letting my mind wander, I thought back to the image from the migraine. Had I met Emmerich before? Or was it just a desire I had, to be close with him and for us to learn about the universe together? I loved sci-fi, it must have just been a desire.

But it felt so real.

Reaching for my necklace, which I always did when I was stressed or pondering, I found it missing. I shot up, head pounding, and kept feeling around for it. It was gone. It was the only thing I had from my past, I couldn't just lose it. Did I put it in my backpack? Quickly, I fumbled through my bag but found nothing. The knot must have come loose either at school or on my way back.

I grabbed my keys and ran out of my apartment. I had to find it. Deciding to retrace my steps, I headed toward the MAX. If all else failed maybe someone turned it in to the lost and found at school. Worse-case scenario, I had lost it on the MAX and the odds of someone finding it and turning it were close to zero.

The necklace wasn't that special in and of itself. It was just a simple piece of wood with my name carved in it. It was how the doctors had known my name. How I found my name. I had tried to find someone who could tell me what type of wood it was. No one knew. Most thought it was some kind of fake man-made wood.

I made it back to PCC and scanned the concrete as I slowly stepped forward. Students bumped into me as they raced by to get to class. I must have looked insane but I had to be thorough, making sure I had checked every inch.

Reaching the lab room, some students were still finishing up their lab for the later section. The TA, Kim, was helping one of the students.

"Um, Kim," I began.

She turned around. "Yes, Angela was it?"

I nodded. "Yeah, but I seemed to have lost my necklace. Did anyone turn it in?" I hoped for a yes but the look on her face told me she didn't know what I was talking about.

She shook her head. "Sorry, dear, I haven't seen it. You can look around if you want."

I sighed. "All right, thanks."

I scanned the area where Emmerich and I had been working. Nothing. I went to the lost and found on the other side of campus. That too was a bust.

With my head hanging low, I started back toward my apartment. The one thing I had of my past and I had lost it. Tears were forming in my eyes. I felt like such a child, starting to cry because I had lost something so small. But I had never lost something so important before.

I wiped the tear that dripped down my face. I had to keep up hope, someone might find it and turn it in. Why would anyone want a piece of jewelry that had someone else's name on it? It wasn't even that fancy, all it was made of was wood and leather string.

"Angela!"

I turned to find Emmerich jogging towards me, his light blonde hair even brighter in the sun shining on this crisp, clear day. In his hand he held up my necklace. I could tell even from a distance. I cleared away the tears and hurried to him.

"I found it on the floor of the lab. I tried to run after you but you were long gone. I'm so glad I bumped into you."

"Thank you so much, I don't know what I would have done if I didn't find it," I tied it around my neck, double checking the knot. My eyes were probably still red from the tears. I sniffled and wiped my face again.

"It's no problem, I forgot something in the lab and saw

it on the ground. If all else failed, I knew I could give it to you on Monday."

"That was really sweet of you, I'm so happy you saw it."

"It must be special to you if you were this worried about it."

"You have no idea," I mumbled. I didn't want to go into detail standing in the middle of campus. "Is there any way I can repay you?"

He grinned, showing off his perfect teeth. "How about you let me treat you to some coffee? Coffehouse-5 isn't too far from here."

I stared up at his crystal blue eyes. First, he finds my necklace, and now he's asking me out? This was too perfect. "I think that would be fair."

Emmerich led the way. Coffeehouse-5 was a small café across from the university that most students went to. It was local, so many people liked it for that, and they also had some awesome cups they served with. I usually went to cafés downtown on my way to school, so I hadn't gone to this place that often.

We didn't say much on the way there, me being shy and him trying to make a path through all the students on the sidewalk. I was glad he was leading, otherwise I would run into people or just not getting around as fast. I really hated crowds even though I lived in the city. Emmerich, on the other hand, seemed used to it and went through the crowd with ease.

Making it to the café, we got into the massive line that almost reached the doors to the outside. I was glad we were at least inside the café as it was cold out.

"So are you interested in astronomy or are you just taking an easy elective?" Emmerich asked as we stepped in line.

I shrugged. "I like it a lot and took last term's section. So, it's at least one of my interests for the time being."

He laughed. "Too many interests? I can relate."

"More or less just trying to find what my true interests are."

"Been there too. Life's complicated like that, leading us to believe we like one thing but in reality, there's something out there that we could love more. We just haven't found it yet."

"Exactly." The line shifted forward slowly.

I glanced around at the different pictures. "These are some amazing photographs, don't you think?"

He looked up. "Yeah, they are pretty talented artists."

I swayed back and forth on the balls of my feet. "Which one is your favorite?"

Emmerich's eyes darted back and forth between the photographs. "That one there." He pointed. I looked over to find the one he liked was of a Tibetan woman standing in front of her village, as if waiting for something. "It captures her soul, I think, showing how life truly is like for her. My guess is she is the leader of the tribe, working to keep her people on their feet."

"Have you been there? To Tibet, I mean."

He laughed. "No, I haven't. It's a bit hard to get into any of those regions unless you are a true adventurer. What about you, which is your favorite?"

"That one." I pointed at a beautiful cityscape that looked almost sci-fi.

"Ah, Hong Kong. Quite a unique place. The cityscape is said to be the best on Earth," he replied.

I nodded. "It's beautiful, especially with the water surrounding it. It reminds me of..."

"Of what?"

I blinked, realizing I had trailed off. My cheeks reddened. "Sorry, I didn't mean to do that. There's something about it that makes me smile."

He turned back to the photo. "Well, it is a beautiful place. I would love to go some day."

"Me too."

At last we made it to the front of the line and the

barista took our orders. Emmerich asked for a white mocha and I got a caramel macchiato. I knew that was what everyone ordered, but I loved it anyway, especially when they put in extra caramel. Emmerich told her the order was for here and I just hoped we could find a seat. Luckily, as we turned around, a couple got up to leave.

Emmerich took a sip of his white mocha. "What were your interests growing up?"

That was the question, wasn't it? Usually I made up some lie when people asked about my past. But for some reason, I couldn't lie to him. "That's the funny thing, I don't remember. I was found about a year ago with no memory of my past. No one around knew who I was, and I can't track down anything about myself."

I studied his reaction. When I revealed that information to people their immediate response was pity and sorrow, as if I was the saddest thing they had ever heard. Some of my students' parents even gave me more money than I asked for. I didn't complain about that, though, I needed it. Emmerich's reaction was different. Most people's bodies tensed but I could see his shoulders relax and he seemed... relieved to hear the information. I wasn't sure how to take that.

He adjusted himself in his seat and I realized I was studying him. I hope I didn't make him feel uncomfortable, even though I found his reaction to be strange. I tensed up, eager for his response and wondered if he would make some excuse to run off. "I'm sorry to hear that, I didn't mean to bring up any hurtful memories. I had no idea."

"It's fine," I interrupted before he could go on. I didn't need to hear the same words everyone had said, and I was happy he didn't make some lame excuse to leave. "What about you, though? Your accent sounds German, how long have you been in the states?"

His left eyebrow went up. "How can you tell? Most can't place it since it has mixed with..." he stopped and coughed. "Other places I have been."

I shrugged. "I just knew. It seemed..." I laughed. "You will think I'm strange, but I swear I've heard your voice somewhere before."

His eyes shined for a moment, then he coughed into his sleeve. "Maybe we bumped into each other in the street once."

I wrinkled my nose. That wasn't it, at least that's not what my gut said. I didn't push it further, though. I didn't want to seem like a stalker, or seem like I thought him a liar. Maybe we hadn't met before and I didn't want to ruin a possible relationship with just a hunch.

I changed the topic back to school. "Did you come here

as an exchange student?"

He rubbed his chin. "Yeah, I did, in high school. I have been here a while now, I'm surprised you could pick up the accent. Thought it was mostly gone now."

I traced the rim of my half-empty cup with my finger. "Well, don't lose it, I think it gives you more character."

He chuckled. "I've been told that before."

I hoped he didn't mean by a girlfriend or something, my heart would have stopped right then and there if he did. There was a connection between us, that was clear. I never felt so open with someone and he seemed to be open with me as well. Is this what it felt like to have a crush on someone?

"So, what are your interests?" I asked, realizing we had been mostly talking about me.

"Astrobiology. I also like theoretical physics—whether other dimensions exist and if we can travel through the dimensions to reach other galaxies."

I perked up. "Is that possible?"

"It could be." He let out a brief sigh. "But that's for graduate school. Now I'm just trying to do smaller research projects and pass my classes."

I nodded. I knew how he felt. Dreams of the future but stuck in the present. "Me too."

"What kind of research would you want to do, if given

the chance?"

"I don't know yet, probably something to do with space travel or the multi-verse." I placed my hands on the table and leaned back. "I admit it, I'm obsessed with *Doctor Who*."

"Is that still running?"

I tilted my head. "What do you mean, still?"

His eyes darted away from mine for a second then shrugged. "I used to watch it then I veered off onto something else. I thought they ended the show. I'm just out of the loop I suppose."

"Oh, where did you leave off?" I asked, excited about finding someone else who had seen the show.

"With the eleventh doctor, but my favorite is nine. I just liked his attitude and sass a bit more."

I smiled as I lifted my mug. "Me too! The new doctor is doing a pretty good job but I still think nine is the best too. Ten is a close second, but definitely like David Tennant as an actor more."

"Then there's always Captain Jack."

I choked on my coffee. Captain Jack was definitely a wild character. I set my mug down. "I love the episodes he guest stars in, I haven't gotten to Torchwood yet."

"It's not bad, darker than Doctor Who."

"I must check it out then." I took another sip of my

caramel macchiato. "So, what other shows do you watch?"

"I, uh, haven't been watching much television. I used to watch *Eureka* and *Warehouse 13*, but that was a while back. How about you?"

"Haven't seen those. I just follow *Doctor Who* and *Grimm* right now. I started *Vampire Diaries* this week. Still deciding if I like it or not. Everything's new to me so it's all overwhelming," I explained, wishing I could take back the last part. I hated saying things like that, it made things awkward.

He was silent for a moment, as if thinking of a way to respond. "That must be strange, having to relearn everything like that. At least you're never bored."

"When you put it that way, yes, every day seems like an adventure," I glanced up at the entrance as the two men in black walked in. It was The Brothers. They looked straight at us. I started gathering my things. "I should get back to my apartment, I have a lot of things to do."

"How about I walk you home?" He stood up and grabbed his coat.

Did I hear him right? Did he really want to walk me home? Even without the scary men at the door it was an automatic yes. "I live downtown though."

"That's okay, I need to go there today, anyway."

I kept my head down as Emmerich led me out of the coffee shop and out of sight of those men. He didn't seem to have noticed them, maybe I was just overreacting, and they were just a few normal Portlanders.

That I seemed to keep running into this week.

"So, to the MAX then?" he asked.

I nodded. "Yeah, it's this way." I led him down the street toward the station. I was glad my headache had gone away after I took my herbs so I could enjoy this. I felt familiar and happy with him at my side, especially with those guys hanging around.

Just as we got to the station, the MAX came, and we had to run and jump on before it left, otherwise we would have to wait another fifteen minutes. We were both laughing, adrenaline rushing and out of breath.

"I always hate it when I get to the station with only seconds to spare, it's so stressful," I said as we grabbed a seat.

"Yeah, I know what you mean, especially when you are with another person. I'm always afraid of getting separated."

"Oh, I never thought of that. That would be scary too."

He laughed. "Yeah, I have had it happen to me before too, in Berlin. I got separated from my mutter and schwester when I was little. I freaked out and cried a lot."

"Oh, that is so sad. I'm sorry."

Emmerich waved it off. "It's fine, it was a long time ago. I found my mother and sister with the help of a policeman."

"Well, I'm glad you were fine."

I glanced outside and saw The Brothers on the street. So, they headed to the MAX station just like us. I tried not to stare, but they were freaking me out, and it looked like they saw where I was on the MAX.

"Is there anything wrong? You seem nervous," Emmerich asked.

"It's nothing, I just thought I saw someone I knew but it wasn't them," I lied. "Is Germany like Oregon?" I changed the subject and had no clue if it was, I hadn't had a conversation with anyone from a different country before. All I knew was from TV and the internet, but that didn't give a feel of a place, just the facts, and sometimes not even those.

"In scenery, it is similar, but the city structure is different. The lack of public transportation in the United States is outstanding."

"Really? What's it like over there?"

He paused, as if trying to recall the memories. "Quite nice. We have a subway system in most cities and buses that are a lot more organized."

"Where in Germany are you from?" Not that I knew the country very well. Heck, all I knew about Germany was that it was next to France.

"München—Munich. It's a great place, really. I miss it a lot."

For a moment he seemed to go back into his thoughts. It was like he was somewhere else—maybe he missed his home more than he was letting on. "Then why did you leave?"

Emmerich shrugged. "Good question. Just wanted to try something new I suppose. I liked the idea of coming here to study. An adventure of sorts. The goal is to go to PSU or OSU for physics."

I stretched my arms up at the sky. "That sounds amazing. I would give anything to just leave and have an adventure. I'm stuck here until then."

"That's what's great about adventures, you never know when the next one will come," he said as we reached the apartment. Emmerich went ahead and walked me up the stairs. Once we were at the door, I thanked him again for the coffee and for finding my necklace.

"You don't happen to have anything going on tomorrow, do you?" he asked as he leaned against my doorway.

I had to think of what day it was. Today was Friday so

tomorrow had to be Saturday. My first weekend. "I have to tutor three kids tomorrow, but the first one isn't until two. I'm free all morning."

He beamed. "Good, do you want to go to the Saturday Market in the morning? We could pick up some crêpes for breakfast and then venture around."

"Crêpes?"

"Like a very thin pancake with fruits or other filling," he explained. I was glad he didn't make fun of me not knowing. Sometimes I remembered foods but other times I was clueless.

"That sounds great," I said. Truly, it did. I wondered why I hadn't come across the food before, as I had gone to the Saturday Market enough times.

"Great, I'll pick you up at ten. See you tomorrow."

With that, he left me at my doorstep. As I unlocked my door, I felt my heart racing. There was no way I would sleep tonight.

I woke up before my alarm clock went off. It was astonishing that had never happened before. I had set it for eight and I was up by seven. I guess I didn't hate mornings when I had something to look forward to.

Or someone.

I was giddy with everything I did to get ready for the

date. Was it a date? Why else would he have asked to go to the Saturday Market with me? Yes, it had to be one.

Turning up the speakers of my computer, I blasted Marian Call's album "Something Fierce" as I took a long, hot shower, thinking of how glorious the day would be. Nothing could go wrong, I wouldn't allow it.

Which meant something would go wrong.

The song "Dear Mr. Darcy" began, one of my favorites. I used my shampoo bottle to lip sync to the song.

And you said I was sweet, nearly kissed me goodnight,

And it was almost perfect, but -- not -- quite --

A song about an awkward encounter between a guy and a girl, it was perfect for me. I rinsed the conditioner out of my hair as the song ended. I was so ready for the day.

As I stepped out of the shower, I glanced at the clock. Still only fifteen after eight. I had plenty of time to pick the perfect outfit and get my hair to look how I wanted it, or at least close. My hair never looked how I wanted it, I swore. The music still played from the bathroom.

But if ever love astounds you, you have to let it, have to let it

Oh if ever joy surrounds you, you have to let it, have to let it

Oh if ever love astounds you, you have to let it, have to

let it

I settled on a pink and red flowery blouse with some worn-out jeans. And, of course, white Converse. I didn't wear any other shoe. I found them to be one of the best shoes ever, after putting in a gel support. Although they weren't that warm in the winter months.

Now the makeup and hair. I put a little bit of a curl into my hair and it looked a lot better than I expected it to. After another half an hour, I was ready for Emmerich to pick me up. I checked the time on my fox watch. Fifteen until ten. Good thing I woke up early.

Right on time, I heard a knock on the door. I opened the door to find Emmerich in a jean jacket and a band shirt. Oomph!. I would have to check them out when I got back.

"Guten Morgen."

"Morning," I grinned.

We stood there in awkward silence for a moment. "Well, shall we go?" he asked as he motioned down the hallway.

"Yeah, of course," I locked the door behind myself.

"Who's this, deary?" Ms. Collins stepped out into the hallway.

Oh great. "This is Emmerich, he's from Germany. We are running late though, so I have to go."

Emmerich waved to her. "Hello."

She gave him a fishy look, then thankfully went back into her apartment.

I let out a sigh. "Sorry about that, she enjoys checking up on me for some odd reason. It's kind of creepy and cute at the same time."

"That's no problem," he laughed. "Reminds me of my grandmother, actually."

Heading out into the street, Emmerich turned to me. "So how has your morning been?"

I shrugged. "All right, I suppose as mornings can go. Better now though."

He stuck his hands into his pocket. "Better now that you're with me?"

"Maybe, we will see how the day goes."

"So, I'm being critiqued then?" He raised an eyebrow.

I shoved him playfully. I already felt comfortable with him. It was strange, I had never felt this way with someone before. Was it because he was the first person to truly accept me? Or was there something more to it?

The Saturday Market was down by the waterfront, sort of close to Voodoo Donuts. I thought about mentioning donuts to Emmerich but remembered he was going to introduce me to crêpes. I just hoped that they were as great as donuts.

It was interesting that I could remember some foods but not others. Donuts, I remembered vaguely, but as to these crêpes, I had no idea what they were. I also had never remembered ham and bacon and I didn't care for it.

People were already out in droves. Good thing I didn't mind crowds. In fact, sometimes I felt more comfortable around lots of people. Don't get me wrong, I liked my solitude from time to time, but everyone has a story and I enjoyed watching to see what that is.

The market was full of homemade, unique goods. There was probably everything from food to tie-dyed shirts to Native American rugs. If you couldn't find it here, then it wasn't worth buying. Also, here, everything was homemade and very... unique. After passing a booth with steampunk gnomes, I found the word "unique" definitely applied.

Emmerich led me to the little vendor that sold crêpes and, after a ten-minute wait, they were wrapped up and handed to us. I had ordered a strawberry cream, and he had ordered a cinnamon honey banana.

After one bite, I was in love. Light and fruity, they seemed healthier than a donut. I had a new favorite breakfast and snack—and the whipped cream inside was an added bonus. I wondered how easy they were to make. It didn't seem too hard, if one had the right pan.

"Where would you like to go first?" he took a bite of his crêpe, honey smeared the edges of his mouth.

I laughed and wiped it away with my napkin. "Always such a messy eater."

"What?" He looked at me.

I blinked. Why had I said that? I've never seen him eat before. "I... I don't know where that came from, sorry," I glanced around. "How about we start over there?"

After staring at me a moment longer, he nodded. "Let's go."

We wandered into the part where all the photographs were sold—pictures that made you want to travel the world to places like Italy, Japan, China, France. Hidden amongst the hundreds, I noticed one of Germany.

I pointed at the photo. "Have you been here?"

He squinted as he read the caption underneath. "Lindau, Germany. Ja, I've been there. I used to go every summer with mutter. Been a while though."

I admired the photo more. "It looks beautiful. How often do you fly back?"

He frowned and scratched his head. "I haven't been back in a few years. I came here and I guess I just never looked back."

I turned back to the painting. "I don't know how you could leave such a place behind. And your family..."

"It's a lot easier than you'd think," he mumbled. "Shall we move on? There's a lot more to explore?"

I nodded. "Sure."

We ventured to the other side of the market. People sold all different types of artwork, ranging from playing cards to art made of garbage, to clown masks. I shuddered. I hated clowns, they freaked me out.

We turned down toward a circle of tents. Trinkets from China filled many of the booths. Plushies of Pikachu and Sailor Moon—two pop culture icons recognizable even to me—hung up on the walls. Further down a woman sat alone. Her greying blonde hair was pulled back in a bun and her narrow fingers tapped a deck of cards on the table. Her blue eyes looked wise but still full of youthful energy, belying the wrinkles on her face.

She pointed at me and motioned for me to come closer. "I will read your fortune for only five dollars. Please come sit, I am very good."

When someone says they're good at something, it's almost guaranteed to be a lie.

I turned to Emmerich. He shrugged. "It's fine by me if you want to try it."

Pulling out five dollars, I put it on the table and sat down.

"Give me your hand." She grasped my hand with her

cold hands and closed her eyes. "I see... a dark shadow lingering over your past, as if you are hiding something. The deeper you go, the darker it is. It's hard to see anything behind you," she paused, searching for more.

How did she know that everything seemed to be hidden from me? My heart raced, eager to hear more.

"You and this young man go way back. You are connected—always meant to be together," she said. "Destiny has brought you to each other against all odds. The universe can't keep you apart."

Well, that got awkward fast. First date and a psychic says we are meant to be. I glanced over at Emmerich but he just stared at the lady, frowning.

"There's more. You are an important person. Very important. I don't know how, but all the answers will be revealed to you soon." She opened her eyes. "Now, I will read your fortune with my cards."

She shuffled the cards and laid them out on the table. "This card is your present, this is your past." She flipped over another card. "This is your fears and this is your joys." She flipped over the last card. "And this is your future." She read the cards carefully, nodding to herself. "Very interesting indeed. The Magician. You are a smart woman, searching for answers in everything that you do. As for your past..." She touched the card.

"The Eight of Swords tells us of a loss of control. You feel you can't grasp your former life. Nine of Swords, you fear your lingering thoughts will leave you hopeless. You need to move away from them and enjoy life. Your joys—" she smiled and glanced at Emmerich. "Include a lover and you should be open to any proposals that come your way." She looked at the last card and frowned. "Ten of Swords. Disaster is coming your way. You must prepare for the fight ahead of you."

"The fight?"

The psychic's eyes seemed to look through me. "There is a war that has been going on for a long time. You must prepare and draw your sword. Trust those near you as they have your back." She blinked and turned to Emmerich. "Would you like your fortune told as well?"

"No thank you, I think we better get going. Come on Angela." He held out his hand and helped me up.

"Thank you!" I waved at the fortune teller as we left her booth. I turned to Emmerich. "Well, that was odd, huh?"

"Yeah, I buy very little into that sort of thing," Emmerich seemed to keep looking back behind himself.

I went on. "She got my past right though, that's a bit strange."

"It's the Forer effect, saying things that are broad

enough that anyone can relate." He tried to sound casual to diffuse the awkwardness, but my heart felt like it would drop out of my chest.

"Yeah, I guess that's true," I looked up at the sky and took in the beautiful blue color. Even though it was chilly, today I could see the sun, and that made me happy. An adventure sounded wonderful, even if it would be a hard fight. "Too bad, I was looking forward to this war of hers. Sounds, sci-fi-ish, you know? Like Doctor Who," I laughed.

Emmerich said nothing. I guess he was embarrassed about all that "meant to be" stuff. He seemed more frustrated, his fists were clenched and his body tense. He looked back again, as if searching for something. Maybe he had seen someone he didn't want to run into and that was why he was in such a rush.

I glanced back, a man in black was staring right at me. It was Scarface, who I admit, was the scariest of the five men I had run into this past week. He was grinning, and it gave me the shivers. He didn't move but just stood there as if trying to scare us. Looking up at Emmerich, I wondered if it had anything to do with him.

"You don't happen to know that man over there, do you? The one with the scar" I nodded over at him. I didn't want to point in fear that he might move toward us.

He looked over at the man. "Oh, him?" He paused like he was trying to come up with an answer. "Yeah, that's George, one of my brother's friends."

That was obviously a lie, not to mention that man did not look like a George. Maybe a Steve. He also never mentioned a brother. And the fact I doubted he had family in the area since he said they were all back in Germany. "Then why are we heading away from him? Shouldn't you talk to him?"

"It's just a game we play, don't worry about it. You're perfectly safe with me."

Why would I worry that I wasn't safe with him? He was leading me away from the scary man so I wasn't going to complain. I wanted answers, but I hesitated to ruin a perfectly good date. I would ask him later.

"So, where to next?" I asked with a smile, hoping he would forget about the fortune teller, and the man watching us. Although, maybe I didn't want him to forget about the man, then he wouldn't be ready if he decided to follow us.

He pondered for a moment. "Hm... I don't care, where do you want to go?"

I thought for a second. Then it hit me, the perfect place to go on a date. "Have you been to the Lan Su Chinese Garden?"

He shook his head. "No, where is that?"

"You have to go. It's this way! Come on." I grabbed his arm and pulled him toward Portland's Chinatown.

The gardens were only a few minutes away. Emmerich didn't protest as I kept my arm entwined with his. He didn't say much but seemed to be in a better mood now that we were away from the marketplace.

On the way I checked to make sure the man was no longer following us. I tried not to think about it, not wanting to spoil the fun of being on a date with such a cute guy, even though he was keeping something from me. Didn't everyone have secrets though? Maybe not the same but there are always things people don't want others to know.

At Lan Su I paid the student entrance fee. Emmerich tried to give me money but I insisted that I owed him for both the crêpes and the coffee, not to mention finding my necklace. After a minute of arguing, he gave in.

Walking through the archway was like being transported into another world. Classic Chinese architecture blocked out the modern world, other than the tops of the few skyscrapers Portland possessed. If I wanted a day away, I would either come here or go up to the Portland Rose Gardens, or the Oregon Zoo. The zoo was just fun and I always tried to imagine what the animals were like in the wild.

The cherry trees looked as if they couldn't wait for spring when their buds would blossom. I admit, this wasn't the best time to go to a garden, but the energy surrounding the place was great. And I could then comment that we should come back in the spring.

"Well, what do you think?" I watched his face.

He looked around, wide-eyed. "This place is wunderbar, I can't believe I've never been. The architecture and plants make it feel like I'm not even in the city."

I stood tall, satisfied with the response. "I'm glad you like it."

He grabbed my hand, and we strolled along a path made of large rocks. His skin felt warm against mine and I wanted to hold his hand forever. The fortune teller was right, this was one of my joys.

We bought some food to feed the koi and threw a couple of cheerios in at a time, I leaned against the support beam and looked down at our reflection.

"Where do you see yourself in the future?" I asked.

He shrugged. "I always saw myself getting a PhD in physics and moving back to Germany, but that all changed."

"What do you mean?"

Emmerich looked at me with his bright blue eyes. "Someone made me change my mind. Showed me that a purpose is more important than individual goals. Physics was something I wanted to do, but I learned there were other things in life that were more important."

"Well that person sounds amazing. I wish I could meet them."

"She is and I would do anything for her," he laughed as if it was a joke I wasn't in on. I felt my heart race. He had said 'her.' Were they once an item? "What about you, where do you see yourself?"

I leaned back and looked up at the sky. "I guess it all depends on the present." And whether the fortune teller was right about the war and finding love. "But finding purpose for others sounds like a good dream."

He watched me with a gentle smile on his face. I thought about asking why he was looking at me like that, but I didn't want to ruin the moment. I dropped some more cheerios into the pond, watching the small waves appear before the koi dissolved it away with their own movements. One of the koi splashed us, hitting Emmerich right in the face. I laughed as he wiped it away with his sleeve.

"That was disgusting." He spat into the water.

"Maybe you weren't feeding him fast enough."

"I guess. That fish just needs to calm down."

We both chuckled at the comment and finished feeding the fish in companionable silence. I watched as the koi nibbled, pushing each other out of the way for more. I loved the different colors they had, not just orange, but black, and white speckles as well.

I checked my watch. It was thirty minutes until two. I needed to get back. "I should probably head to my tutoring session."

Emmerich jumped down from the rock. "I'll walk you there. Where do you need to go?"

"Just over to Powell's Books. You don't need to walk me, it's fine. Kind of out of the way."

He put his hand in mine, intertwining our fingers. "It's all right, I want to."

I leaned my head against his shoulder as we left the garden. This was the perfect day. It felt comfortable. It felt safe. It felt...

Familiar?

It happened again, some images started to form in my mind. Emmerich and I strolled together, through a garden just like this. It was different though, none of the trees and plants were the same. They didn't look like anything of this world. Emmerich was wearing some type of suit, and I was wearing a yellow summer dress. We were laughing, having a good time. It was before the darkness. It was before that day...

I knelt down and grabbed my head, instinctively reacting in pain. The migraine had come back.

"Are you okay?" Emmerich placed his hands on my arms, helping me back up.

"Yeah, I just..." I looked up at him, debating if I should tell him what I saw. It was the second time I had a vision of him. "I just need some water. Can we stop there?" I pointed at a small café. People were staring at us as Emmerich helped me up.

He nodded. "Yes, no problem. Let's get you inside."

Emmerich got me a water, and I gulped it. The pain went away slowly, and we started again for the bookstore.

I thought about the vision. It was definitely Emmerich standing with me. We were enjoying ourselves at some party. Was it a banquet? It looked nothing like Portland. Did Emmerich know where I was from? If so, he made no comment about it. If he knew, wouldn't he have said something? And where could I find that yellow dress? It looked so cute on me.

"How often do you get spells like that?"

"Until this week, never. I probably will go to a doctor next week."

"I hope everything is okay."

I shook my head, waving off the thought. "It's fine, I should be fine. Probably just too much fun for one day. Don't worry about it."

"Are you sure?" he asked one last time, looking at me, concerned.

I nodded. "But I was wondering about that guy back at the farmer's market. He's just your brother's friend?"

"Yeah, just a friend."

"I've seen him around, more than once. In fact, that was the third time I've seen him this week," I went on.

"Did you run into me around the same time?"

I thought back to it. I had seen Emmerich around when those men showed up. "So, they have been looking for you?"

"Yeah, just some old friends in town. I hope they didn't scare you, I'm sorry if they did."

I waved it off. "No, no. I just found it strange that I kept running into them. Now I know they were just looking for you."

"Yup."

We reached Powell's and Emmerich kissed my hand. "Feel better. Promise me you will go straight home afterward."

I smiled. "I will. Maybe see you tomorrow?"

"I'll stop by in the afternoon. I promise."

With that, he left me to meet with my student. The first one for the afternoon, Katelynn, was already waiting for me. I sat down next to her at the table.

"Sorry I'm a little late," I brushed a piece of my ginger hair out of my face. "How's biology been going?"

"It's going, but let's talk about chemistry." She leaned forward with a grin. "Who was that hunk? Is he your boyfriend?"

I blushed. "He might be."

"Well, did he ask for your digits at least?"

I was taken aback by the question. I never thought about exchanging cell numbers because I never used my cell phone. But why didn't he ask for mine? Isn't that what everyone does nowadays?

As promised, I went straight back to my apartment. The headache had gone away but I could still feel the lingering numbness. I would take another dose of my herbal concoction. It worked wonders.

When I got home, I collapsed. Three tutoring sessions back to back was exhausting. Especially after spending the whole morning with Emmerich.

I let my thoughts drift back to him. He was perfect. I hoped I didn't screw this one up. I had almost forgotten, I would check out Oomph!. I typed it into my iTunes and hit play for the first track that was in English, "Labyrinth".

KNOCK KNOCK LET ME IN,
LET ME BE YOUR SECRET SIN,
LEFT, RIGHT, STRAIGHTAHEAD,
YOU'RE IN THE LABYRINTH

I shut it off quickly. I didn't see Emmerich being a metal fan. That was not my scene, I was more of a folk music kind of girl. I glanced at the microwave to see it count down its last four seconds. Grabbing a spoon, I took my soup out of the microwave and turned on my laptop to get on Netflix.

Tonight I would watch *Torchwood*.

A loud thumping at my door made me just about jump out of my bed. I looked at the clock. Just past two in the morning. Darkness surrounded me as the door shook with every pounding that it took. I could hear it creak under the pressure. My poor door.

I grabbed the metal bat next to my bed and slipped on some sandals. If I had to run, I wanted shoes on. I had watched too many shows where someone got caught because they couldn't run anymore on their cut-up bare feet. I was strange but I wasn't stupid.

I looked through the peephole. Two men in suits standing outside, trying to force their way into the apartment. It was Beardy and Muscleman. Where were the other three? Why didn't they ever show up all together? Wouldn't that just be easier?

None of my neighbors seemed to care that my door was being broken down. Figures. That's what happens when you stay in an apartment downtown, no one notices loud noises and Ms. Collins took out her hearing aids at night. Everyone else was probably all wasted and wouldn't wake up. That was probably it, it was Saturday night. From Thursday night to Monday morning, everyone on this floor was wasted. Sometimes Wednesday. I learned that the hard way.

Debating what to do next, I checked my surroundings. I didn't have a fire escape, and I was three floors up. I couldn't jump down unless I wanted to break something or test the possibility that I could fly. No, not today. The only way out was through the front door.

Quickly, I grabbed my phone and called Detective Johnson. After four very, very slow rings, he answered the phone.

"Hello?" He sounded tired, but he still answered.

"There's someone trying to break into my apartment!" I screamed.

"Angela, is that you?" He sounded more alert.

"Yes! Yes, it is! Beardy and Muscleman are trying to break my door down!"

"Wait, who?" he muttered something else under his breath. "Never mind, I'm sending men there right now, I will be there shortly. Don't worry, we are coming."

"What do I do in the meantime?" I tried taking a deep breath to stop panicking but it didn't help. I was panicking.

"Do you have any weapons?" he asked. I heard sirens coming from the distance. He worked fast.

"I have a bat."

"Well, if you need to, use it. My men are almost there, just hang on and stay on the line..."

As if they knew it was their cue, my door crashed down, splinters shattering throughout my apartment. I dropped the phone, the battery shot out like a torpedo. I stared at the phone for a moment, the world seeming like it had stopped. Crap, I needed that. There was no time to lose, I had to protect myself now.

I grabbed my bat with both hands. Muscleman lunged at me and I swung right into his chest. It knocked the wind out of him and he stumbled back. As quickly as I could, I ran at Beardy. He didn't see it coming, and I knew that. I smashed the bat into his head and ran out into the hallway.

I hurried out of the building and onto the street, glad that I had put on my shoes because glass littered the sidewalk in front of the building. My breaths were short and quick, my sight blurry from my eyes not resting on something for more than a half-second. I tried to slow down my breathing. I needed to think clearly.

Darkness, just like that night.

I grabbed my head. Not a good time to get a headache. Why was I always so unlucky? I could hear sirens getting closer and saw their lights in the distance. I started toward them, hoping everything was finally all right.

Of course, I was completely wrong about that.

I felt strong arms wrap around my waist. I screamed. They were here, I should have run toward the sirens the moment I stepped out of the apartment. It didn't matter, they probably would have gotten me, anyway. I tried to escape but he was too strong. I bit down onto his hand. I wasn't afraid to fight back, I watched too many shows to not be. He let go only for a second but it was enough for me to get loose. I tried to run but Scarface grabbed me.

"Well, well, what do we have here? Looks like our girl is lost in this strange world. Let us help her get back." He laughed.

Our girl? Lost? What the heck, who were these guys?

I kept fighting, but it was no use, he was a lot stronger than the other men and I had trouble getting out of his grasp. Scarface didn't leave any of his flesh near my mouth, he had seen what happened to one of The Brothers. I didn't stop trying though, I would never stop trying.

"Let go of her!"

Emmerich stepped out of the darkness. Both of The Brothers pulled out guns—at least I think they were guns. They didn't look like any guns I had ever seen. Before they could shoot, Emmerich drew his own. Within seconds the two brothers were dead and Emmerich pointed the gun at Scarface.

Scarface used my body as a shield. "You won't be able to shoot without hitting her. Do you really want to risk that? Not when she means so much."

"It's no risk," Emmerich pulled the trigger and my heart skipped a beat. The man crumpled, dragging me down with him. I shrieked.

Emmerich hurried over to me. "Are you okay?"

I shook my head. "No! What's going on? Why are your brother's friends after me? And how could you just kill them like that?"

He pulled me up. "They aren't my brother's friends, I just didn't want to frighten you. There's a lot to explain but we have no time. We have to go."

"But the police are almost here, they will protect us."

He grabbed my wrist. "No, they don't have any clue of what's going on. They can't help us."

"Are you crazy? They are policemen! We can't just run off."

"They have no jurisdiction where we're going." His voice was no longer soft, but almost strict and in charge.

"What are you talking about?"

"You have to trust me, Angel. You have to come with me."

So many questions ran through my mind, but with everything going on all I could say was, "What?"

"Please, just listen to me. I want to help. I can take you somewhere safe. Somewhere far from here."

I knew I shouldn't listen to him, that it would be safer and smarter to wait for Detective Johnson, but there was a feeling in my gut that told me Emmerich was speaking the truth. With all the flashbacks that had been happening, I knew he would not hurt me. I knew I could trust him. Maybe it was the words 'somewhere far from here' or maybe it was something the fortune teller said, but against my better judgment I agreed. "Okay."

Emmerich pulled me toward the alleyway just as Beardy and Scarface flew out the front door of the apartment building, guns at the ready. Two police cars pulled up, and I saw Detective Johnson pull his gun. As we lost sight of them, I heard gunfire. I looked back, hoping Detective Johnson was fine.

"Don't worry, he's fine."

I nodded, then realized something. "How did you know what I was thinking?"

He ignored the question and led me down another small side street. If he knew about Detective Johnson, did he know more about me? Was he spying one me? And why wasn't he answering any of my questions?

I stopped dead in my tracks. "No, for once answer my questions Emmerich. How did you know?"

He looked back behind me, fearing that they had been followed. "Angel, this is not the time."

"Tell me now, Rick!"

My demand triggered something in my mind. Another image, but this time I was in a uniform and Rick and another man were there. Something about the other man made me shiver. I ordered Rick to do something for me and as I turned away, he called me "Angel." I left the room and something grabbed me...

The image faded away and pain swept through my head. My knees buckled underneath me and I grabbed my head. Emmerich placed his hands on my shoulders.

"Angel, what's wrong? Is it a headache again?"

Although his touch felt warm and comforting, I shoved him back. "Tell me the truth, how do I know you?"

He hesitated. "What... what are you talking about?"

"Don't lie to me, I saw you in a flashback. This is the third time! We were standing on a balcony. You called me Angel, just like you did now. Who are you and what do you want?"

He sighed, as if admitting defeat. "It's a long story, Angel, just trust me. Those men are trying to hurt you and I was sent to protect you. We have to get out of here before they come for us. All I want is you to be safe. I will explain everything once we get to our destination"

"How can I believe someone who has been lying to me?" I asked. Nothing was making sense and my frustration level was through the roof. All I wanted were answers; answers to why he was lying to me and answers to the visions I saw. Were they of my past? Did Emmerich know me back then? Why hadn't he said anything?

"I'm sorry I lied to you but there is a lot going on, given that you don't remember any of it. That you don't even remember who I am." He whispered the last part. "But know I would never hurt you or let harm come to you. I couldn't say anything because I don't know what they gave you to forget. Your head hurts every time you remember something, doesn't it? I'm afraid of what might happen if I tell you the whole story. I have to take you to someone who can figure this out. Do you believe that?" I nodded slowly. "Good, but now we have to go. Can you walk?"

"Yes."

He grabbed my hand, and we hurried back down the street. Few people were out in the dead of night and those who were, were definitely Wesen. I edged closer to Emmerich.

"Where are we going?" my voice sounded more frightened than I had wished.

"Far away from here," he murmured.

I yanked my wrist out of his grasp. "No, you tell me where we are going this instant."

Instead of being mad at me, his face softened. "Always so demanding and stubborn." He shook his head. "But there is no time to explain, not with them on our tails."

"At least tell me why they're after me and why you are helping me."

He looked back behind us, then took a deep breath. "You are a very important person who is feared by very powerful people. They want to kill you because you are the only one who can stop them. I'm protecting you because I'm your friend." He glanced back again. "And want to stop them."

"How can I stop them when I don't even know who they are?"

Emmerich grabbed my hand. "As I said, I will explain once we are safe. Please, just trust me. Just like the fortune teller said."

That was why he had acted so strangely. He knew she was right, there was something bad after me. Did that mean he was here to save me from it? It was just like the fortune teller said. I underestimated her validity.

"As long as you promise to tell me everything."

He nodded. "I will."

We turned down one street then another, and another. I swore we had passed that Starbucks before, but I trusted Emmerich knew where he was going. And besides, there were a lot of Starbucks in Portland. He was probably going around in circles to throw off Beardy and Muscleman. The night was cool, and the moon glowed in the sky. Stars twinkled away and it would have been romantic if it weren't for the fact there were men trying to kill us.

I wondered if Detective Johnson was all right. I really hoped he was, I wouldn't be able to stand him getting hurt because of me. If I left with Emmerich, he would worry. I felt bad, but by Emmerich's look, there wasn't much I could do about that. Emmerich had the answers to my past, I couldn't just let that go, no matter where it took me.

"Where are we going?" I asked after we passed yet another Starbucks. I swear it was the fifth time I had seen it and I was starting to be concerned.

"There's an alley around here somewhere."

Somewhere? I couldn't believe what I heard. "You're lost?"

He shrugged. "Well, I'm not exactly from around here. I went to Oregon State for my PhD."

"PhD? I thought you were an undergrad." Then it hit me, I knew where I had seen him before. "You're that physics student that disappeared a few years back. The police had made me go through all the missing persons reports to see if I had recognized anyone. That's why you seemed familiar before the flashbacks, and why Dr. Moph recognized you too. Your face was plastered all over the TV."

"You caught me, now we have to hurry. Those men are getting closer."

So Beardy and Muscleman had gotten away from the cops. Emmerich quickened his pace but that didn't stop me from asking more questions. "Where did you disappear to? Where have you been for the past three years? And why are you back here?"

"I'll show you in just a moment, if I can just find that damn portal." His eyes scanned forward. "Ah! There it is."

I stopped in my tracks. "Wait, did you just say portal?"

He pulled out a small square device, with three black buttons in the middle. "Yes. Yes I did."

Emmerich pushed the left button and a bright light flashed. Suddenly a giant vertical puddle formed a few feet away. It shimmered in the light, sparkling waves ebbing and flowing. The city behind me reflected off the surface. I could see myself and Emmerich.

And the two men that were following us.

"Rick!" I pointed at the reflection.

The sound of gunshots echoed through the alley. Emmerich pushed me behind a dumpster and pulled out his own gun. I stayed down, trying not to get shot. If I wasn't fearing for my death, I would have asked him about the strange looking gun and why it looked like something from Doctor Who. Then again, so did that large portal that lay before us. Maybe I should question that before I question the guns.

"We have to go through now!" Emmerich ordered.

I looked at the puddle. "I can't go through that, are you

crazy?"

"It's safe, I promise. Now hurry! I will cover you."

I couldn't really argue with what I didn't understand. I sprinted toward the gel-like floating object and halted in front of it.

"Where does it go?"

"It goes home, Angel. You are going home."

"Home?" I opened my mouth to ask where home was, but Emmerich shoved me into it.

An overwhelming tug pulled me into the darkness and I fell for what seemed like an eternity. It was taking me far away, to a different galaxy I somehow knew. A planet light-years from Earth. A place I used to be. A place that....

I still couldn't remember.

The feeling was practically unbearable. A stomach-turning, hair-pulling, gruesome ride that felt like every molecule of my body was being ripped apart and put back together again and again.

A ride that I had been on before.

I had wished for an adventure out of *Doctor Who*, and I'd gotten one. The worst part? I was still wearing pajamas. Pajamas covered in kittens.

Found

I almost threw up everywhere.

Kneeling to the frigid concrete, I took several deep breaths. I couldn't do it—I could not throw up with Emmerich standing next to me. Cute kittens covered the pajamas I wore. If I hurled, I would never forgive myself, much less ever look him in the face again.

Emmerich put his hand on my back. "The feeling will pass—just wait a few seconds."

So he had the same gut-wrenching sensation. Good, I wasn't the only one. I didn't know if the thought of traveling through space made me sick or if it was an obvious side-effect. On TV, the characters had side-effects from such an ordeal, and I had just experienced so much that it wasn't a surprise that the experience made me ill.

Then the past few moments hit me. We had crossed between galaxies in a matter of seconds. How was that logical? This experience reminded me of all the sci-fi movies and books I enjoyed. I couldn't be from a distant world, let alone a different galaxy.

Could I?

This explained why nothing on Earth appeared familiar. My therapist had claimed that in most instances of amnesia the victims lose memories but remember ordinary matters, such as food and books they read. If I didn't come from Earth, it made sense that I recognized nothing and why I swore cars could fly.

I had so many questions to ask Emmerich, but when I opened my mouth, no sounds came out, just the urgency to bring up last night's supper and a handful of popcorn. A little longer and hopefully the feeling would pass.

Emmerich must have suffered from the same problem during his arrival to this place. He traveled to Oregon State University all the way from Germany and ended up in this foreign place. I wondered if his family worried when he went missing. I couldn't imagine. Yet, he remained here. Why?

After a while, my stomach began to feel better. A sour taste still permeated my mouth but at least I knew I wouldn't throw up. I straightened up and dusted off my pajamas, cursing myself under my breath for not wearing something more sensible to bed the night before. At least I had slipped my shoes on before running for my life. I peered up at the area around me and gasped.

We weren't in Portland anymore, that was for sure.

Glass, brick and steel buildings towered over us like titans, I couldn't see the tops of them. Neon lights covered everything—the surfaces of the buildings labeled everything from shops to travel routes. Aircrafts filled the sky, only descending to drop people off before drifting back up into the sky. I wished I could prove everything to my therapist. She assumed the things I told her I recalled were just fantasies or daydreams. Who's making things up now, eh?

The city smelled clean. Portland stunk of fumes, but here the air tasted sweet like a forest or a field of blossoms. Rubbish didn't fill the walkways, no haze to be seen in the distance, the city looked pristine. A few minutes had passed, although it felt longer, as I sat on the sidewalk, peering at the individuals strolling around the city.

They appeared just like those on Earth. Most wore ordinary clothes similar to those on Earth, but a few pieces of attire seemed strange—which scared me considering I lived in Portland. One woman sported an eccentric-fashioned plant bulb on top of her head. A strange vine came whirling out of it, almost striking me in the face as she strode by us. Emmerich pulled me out of the way, but I was too busy collecting in my surroundings to acknowledge him. A group strolled by wearing capes, the breeze causing them to flow in the air. They looked like superheroes, but none of them wore masks. I half wished for a scoundrel to dash past and snatch an aged woman's purse to learn if they would counter. But alas, that didn't happen.

When a young woman wearing a mauve scarf passed us, I peeked at Emmerich but he didn't seem to acknowledge her. Relief overcame me.

I couldn't even describe all the individuals. Hair colors from verdant, to lilac, to navy, every color seemed represented. A lady with rainbow hair passed by and I gawked at her. It was excellent and from what I gathered from having multicolored hair, it was tough to continue looking decent. An old fellow with fire red hair, spiked up like something out of an anime passed me. Individuality was key here. I felt almost like I could live among them, even in my pajamas.

When I peeked up again, an even bigger surprise awaited me. Hidden earlier by the architecture, there, in the sky, hung two giant moons. Yes, two. I didn't even assume they were real for a moment, maybe just a hallucination. I swore I could see structures on both of them, like skyscrapers or resorts. This place really reminded me of Doctor Who. I scanned around again just to make certain no Daleks or Cybermen appeared. I didn't see any but one couldn't be too careful. If I were to see a blue police box, I wasn't certain what I would do.

That's a lie, I would rush straight at it crying for the Doctor.

"That's the same reaction I had when I first saw them," Emmerich said as he too glanced up at the sky. "I couldn't believe they were real."

"People live up there?" I inquired.

He nodded. "Yes, there's an entire metropolis on the moons. A bunch of them are miners since explorers found special minerals on those moons many generations ago. They established a practical process to extricate them and have been doing so since then."

"That's extraordinary," I whispered.

"There are plenty of astonishing things about this

place." He glanced over and grinned. "But we don't have time to go see them all right now."

I still couldn't accept this as reality. I pinched myself, just to make sure. Yup, this was legitimate all right. I was standing on a different planet. Yet it all seemed so...

Normal.

After letting me take all this in, Emmerich grabbed my hand, interlacing his fingers with mine. I felt my cheeks heat from his touch. I turned to him—he looked worried.

"We need to get you somewhere safe, okay? You can't be out in the open like this, they will find you," he said as he pulled me forward.

They? The men that had been chasing us on Earth? I glanced around but didn't see any sign of them. It didn't mean they weren't near. I fiddled with my necklace, feeling the indentation of my name in it. So this necklace was from here.

I didn't know how the portal worked but I hoped it would dump the men out somewhere else in the city. Sometimes portals did that, right? Why else would we be in this part of the city? It made little sense that the portal would open here and not the palace. It must have had some margin of error in where it would dump a person.

Which made it all the more horrifying.

"Who are these people after me and what do they

want?" I asked as we started walking into the crowd.

"They are men sent by an evil person wanting to hurt you. I will explain later the details of that, but first we must get you to safety. Now, don't let anyone see your face. We don't need any unexpected surprises." He took off his jacket. "Here, wear this. You stick out in those pajamas."

I blushed as I put on the jacket. Saying I stood out in the crowd was rather insulting. The jacket itself almost hung lower than my pajama shorts, so I didn't look naked underneath. I hoped Emmerich had some clothes for me to change into wherever we were going. And I hoped they were more sensible than cute little kitten pajamas.

I did as he said and kept my eyes fixed on the concrete beneath my feet. Designs ranging from swirls, to murals, to symbols I didn't recognize covered the cement. Some sidewalks in Portland had similar art, but never this intricate. It was nice to have something beautiful to look at as we rushed through the city.

Emmerich kept his fingers intertwined with mine as we hurried through the streets. I took a deep breath. Emmerich's woodsy yet fruity scent emanated from the jacket, comforting me. Even though we were still in danger, I felt safe with him, as if he could save me from anything. Why, I wasn't sure. I had only just met him a week ago, at least that I could remember. Memories came back to me in pieces hinting that I had known him before the accident, but I had yet to put it all together.

Although Emmerich had told me to keep my head down, I couldn't help but glance at all the extraordinary things around me. We hurried by shops selling different food, beverages, clothing, pets... I swore I saw a dragon in one window, a real live dragon. It was small, red, and in a birdcage. There was even a rabbit in the cage next to it. Strange how some things were the same but others much, much different. It must have been normal because Emmerich didn't even glance at it. Even if it was normal, how could you not stare at it?

Emmerich pushed my head down. "Keep your face from being seen, bitte," he whispered, slipping into German. Although I don't remember learning any of the language, I could always understand him. I must have studied German before losing my memory. I had heard of cases where people have woken up and spoken in a new language. That would have been interesting.

I did as he said, but he never removed his hand for a moment. I knew he worried about someone seeing me, but having his hand against my neck was very uncomfortable. I thought about saying something, but if he didn't want my face to be seen, I doubted he wanted anyone to hear my voice. After a couple more seconds, he took his hand away, for which I was thankful because it relieved the stress from my neck. I did what he wanted and kept my eyes on the ground, watching the different shoes people wore as they went by. So many different shoes.

Was that a giant chicken foot?

I wanted to look up for a second to see the person who went by, if it was a person or a giant chicken. I didn't think it was a giant chicken, but someone in a costume.

Or was it...

It felt like we had been walking for hours, but more realistically, it was more like just twenty minutes. I hoped we were close to wherever we were going. I'd have liked to take a long bath when we got there, but I felt that wouldn't happen. Hopefully I would get to at least take a shower.

We came upon what must have been the food cart district. My stomach started grumbling when the aroma came wafting to me. Maybe Emmerich would stop so we could grab a bite to eat. I had eaten nothing since dinner time and although I wasn't sure what time it was here, my stomach was sure it was time for breakfast. He was in a hurry though, hopefully there would be food where we were going.

A familiar smell. Fire patties. Delicious seasoned meat sliced thin with various corn and peppers, all on a potato patty and covered in hot sauce. I had never eaten them in Portland. I remembered. My stomach grumbled again.

Emmerich chuckled. "Just a bit longer, I promise. We will eat when we get to the base. The guys should have some food."

The guys?

I wanted to ask him who they were, but I figured I wouldn't know who they were, and he won't answer, anyway. I wondered if they were also from Earth or from this world. They must have been from this world since otherwise they would have been with Emmerich. I just hoped they weren't as scary as the men who were after us. I wondered if they would help me remember my past or if they knew my past. I had better get answers when we arrived at the base or else...

Or else what? There wasn't anything I could do. I had nowhere to go, and I had no one except Emmerich. I sighed. There was a lot going on I didn't understand. Once we got to our destination, I would do nothing until Emmerich told me everything.

Turning yet another corner, I noticed it was a lot less crowded here. Emmerich slowed down and didn't seem as worried. "Okay, you can look up now. But keep walking, we don't want to stop."

I raised my head and rubbed the back of my neck. Yup, it would be sore for a couple of days. I tried to pop the vertebrae, but it was no use. I was stuck with the pain for now.

Looking around, this district wasn't as beautiful as the last, grease and grime covered the buildings, bars covered most of the shop windows and doors. The smell was no longer sweet, but stale. It was a big contrast from the streets before, kind of like walking into a different dimension, which I didn't put past this place. We were in the same city, though, I could tell from the buildings. Something must have happened here, something bad to cause such an immense contrast.

I checked down a side street and could see a giant concrete barrier at the end. It was dull and gray and suppressed whatever was on the other side from bystanders. I was curious what they didn't want folks to see. Secret activity? Monsters? Aliens? Whatever it was, it was driving me senseless.

It wasn't there before.

Pain rushed through my skull but I didn't let Emmerich notice. I didn't need him to fret about me when we were on the run, anyhow I was growing used to the burden. Whatever was happening to me, I knew he couldn't help, and I began to wonder if anyone could. Hopefully it would settle itself, but I knew deep down that would not come to pass.

The new vision was of this place, but it was different. It was brimming with life, like the rest of the capital. Rather than the barrier, I noticed an ocean as blue and sparkly as a gem. More splendid than any body of water I'd seen in Oregon. I blinked, coming back to the humdrum reality.

Why was the ocean blocked off from the rest of the city?

If this was my home—and I felt a connection here— the valuable chunks were still missing. I wished it would all come back to me, it would make this a lot easier.

"Why are we here?" I inquired as we wandered further down the street. Almost no crafts flew above us and the characters who remained around watched us with ravenous eyes. I clenched the coat tighter. Emmerich squeezed my hand, letting me know there wasn't anything to worry about.

He maintained his eyes forward, though, not glancing back at me. I assumed he wanted to keep on the lookout in case any of those fellows still wished to strike. "It's fine. Our base is down here."

"Base?" I asked, speculating what he meant by that.

"From there we can figure out what to do," he

revealed, without going into detail.

I looked around again. I couldn't believe his base was in such a run-down place. It didn't seem like a secure place to be, this didn't seem like a decent place for a base of any kind, chiefly if he was trying to protect me. Wouldn't he rather have a military base that was, well, in a better part of town? The people after us looked like the criminals, not Emmerich. Maybe I was wrong, maybe he wasn't who I thought he was.

Why did I have to hide as well? That's what I wanted to understand. How could these simple people recognize me? Maybe he was just more worried that one of the bad guys was in the crowd and would recognize me. There were so many things running through my mind. I hated being in the dark, I wanted to know what to expect.

"What are we going to do next?" I asked, hoping for once he would answer.

"We will talk when we arrive," he whispered.

"Inform me now, Emmerich," I ordered with a lot more authority than I realized I could muster. I stopped going forward and pulled him back. I didn't want to stop in this section, but I felt that the environment would not change. I felt fine as long as Emmerich was with me and since he seemed to be less tense in this area, so did I.

Where did that come from? I wasn't one to make a

command like that, but I suppose I'd never had the opportunity before. I had been on my own for a while.

He spun around and studied me. I expected him to be furious, but Emmerich just grinned. "Such authority, you haven't changed a bit."

Alluding to my history without offering me any information just drove me madder. I wanted to slap him, but concluded that wasn't such a good idea. It was tempting though. "What are you talking about? Why can't you just tell me the truth?" I asked.

He let out a breath. "I didn't plan on you losing your memory. It has complicated matters. I don't know why you don't remember. Was it induced or an accident? I don't know if telling you everything will hurt you or help you," he stepped closer and caressed my cheek. "And I don't know what to say to make you trust me, but realize that I would never harm you. We have a physician at the base that can look you over and later we'll learn more."

I turned, away from his hand. It caused my heart to beat faster, and I had to keep a cool head if I wished to make it through this. "Doctors have examined me, they don't know what's wrong."

He shook his head. "Those are Earth doctors, this is a completely different place."

I took another peek around and observed as a couple

saw us and dashed off in the other direction. Did they recognize us? Or did they not wish to be caught? "Will you at least inform me where we are?"

Emmerich grabbed my hand and launched forward again. It caused me to feel rushed when I really desired to stop for a moment to gather myself. Everything was happening so fast, I could hardly keep up. "Capital City, on the planet Cartref. In the Galaeth galaxy, a completely different galaxy from Earth."

I had guessed we were in a different galaxy, but hearing him say it made my stomach sink. Galaeth he said they called it? It sounded preposterous, but the name seemed so familiar. "But... how?"

"Well, if Earth can develop life, as long as all the criteria are right—," he started.

I shook my head. I understood that part. "No, I mean how are we here? How did we travel lightyears in an instant?"

"Oh, that," he rubbed the scruff on his face. "I may or may not have come across a formula to open a portal while researching dimensional physics."

He made it sound so simple. He must have been quite the genius in college, although most people who studied physics had to be to make it into a graduate program, and, well, pass. "How did you know that a planet would be here?"

"The initial time? I didn't, just figured it out. Verrückt, if you think about it. The odds were not in my favor. The channel between planets stayed open when I traveled back for you, and they continued again when we arrived back."

Verrückt. It meant crazy. I recognized the word. I gawked at him. He didn't know if the portal would work. I didn't know if he was a genius or just idiotic. Probably both, as most scientists were, at least on sci-fi shows.

"So this is where you disappeared to all those years ago? A distant galaxy?"

"Jawohl."

I still wondered what had caused him to remain. Although this place was extraordinary, was it better than his home? I'm uncertain I would give up my home for an adventure. "And this is where I am from?"

He nodded. If it were true, no wonder I couldn't find any record of myself on Earth—because I wasn't even from that planet. It further showed why no one came looking for me until Emmerich. I was grateful that he had found me, even though he wasn't giving me all of the story. There was still one question troubling me more than the others.

"How did I get to Earth?" I asked. "If I am from here,

how did I end up on your world?"

Emmerich pursed his lips, trying to decide how much to reveal me. "Someone kidnapped you. Everyone thought you were dead, but I didn't believe it, you're too resourceful to not escape. But I didn't consider they would take you to Earth, I didn't even think they knew about it. Which makes this more troublesome than I thought it already was..." he drifted off in his thought.

"How is it more troublesome?" I wanted to know. I felt lost already, adding even more to this chaos didn't seem possible.

"Because I thought the only person other than me who knew about it was you. Obviously I was incorrect, which is bad."

So neither planet knew the other existed. I speculated if there were more habitable planets in this system. This place seemed more advanced, but that didn't mean they established their progress into space to colonize planets. I peered back up at the two moons. They seemed inhabited. Colonization of other planets was here.

"So someone else knows about Earth," I affirmed, hoping I wasn't responsible for it.

He nodded. "Ja, and if the wrong people find out, they could bring harm to the world, either side, not to mention the portal is unstable. If used too many times, it could lead to side-effects. Potentially."

That was where theoretical physics always got tricky. Whether playing with the fabric of time and space would lead to the collapse of everything known to man, and then some. "That's... encouraging."

"Well it's hard to know, no one had ever done it before, at least not to my knowledge," Emmerich shrugged. "That's why I never went back, for fear something would go awry when I reopened the portal. Then, when I found it, I realized what must have transpired and came after you."

My mind was scrambling to force the pieces together. Someone had risked creating a portal to force me on Earth. Why? Wouldn't it have been simpler to hide me somewhere on this world? Or kill me? "So you risked everything to bring me back? Why?"

"Because I—" he stopped himself. "You're important and I didn't want to lose you. Not again."

His tone seemed to relax when he talked about his feelings about me. I blushed and struggled not to speculate about his incomplete sentence. "Important? How am I important?"

"After the physician looks at you, I will explain. We are practically there, you won't have to wait much longer."

Even though he had a reason to not tell me, Emmerich didn't understand how disheartening it was not to know who you are. I concluded I may as well change the subject since I would not get any answers soon. I could still see the barrier surrounding us, its somber gray bricks coated with graffiti. "This place used to be thriving. What happened?"

He examined me. "How do you know that?"

I shrugged. "Little things are coming back to me in fragments. I recognize this place and how charming it was."

"Well, it's complicated," he mumbled.

I rolled my eyes. He said that about everything. "Of course it is. That's your answer to everything."

He sighed then nodded to the edge of the city. "Building the wall brought crime to this section. No one wishes to be near it so a lot of the people migrated toward the inner city."

"Why was it built?" I asked.

He laughed. "Now that is a long story."

Why I even bothered asking, I did not know.

"It's true," he stopped in front of a vacated building. I stared up. It looked like all the other buildings in the area, in crappy shape and boarded up with some odd wood. It was like my necklace. I fidgeted with the necklace that still hung around my neck.

A couple of large rat-like creatures scurried around the corner of the building. I let out a small yelp, causing Emmerich to reach for his handgun. When he saw it was just a couple of rodents, he returned to his natural composure and chuckled as he moved his hand away from his gun.

"It's just a couple of rats, nothing to worry about."

I fidgeted with the jacket sleeve. "Didn't say they worried me. I just assumed they would eat me, they were the size of a dog, after all. Just rats you say?"

He shrugged. "Equivalent of a rat here. Could never recall the name."

"Ah, that's... comforting." All I needed to worry about was rodents of unusual sizes running around and nibbling my limbs off. I guess there were drawbacks to this place.

"They won't harm you, if that was what you were speculating. Simply a nuisance. Now as for the horse-sized flies..."

I spun around to face him. "The what?"

"I'm just teasing," he gestured to the building. "Either way, we're here. Remember what I said. No one knows about Earth. Don't mention it to anyone, even if they are on our side. We don't want the knowledge to spread any further."

The door looked weak enough that even I could kick it down, and I feared again what kind of base wasn't secure and seemed desolated. If anyone wished to, they could break in. Why did he think this was safe from those men in black that chased us? I wanted to go someplace else, preferably on the beach with the blue sky above us and white sand under our feet. That would have been a lot nicer than this.

Emmerich pushed part of the wood and the panel came off. He stepped in front of a small scanner on the wall. It looked out of place with everything around it. He opened his eyes wide, and I watched as a bright light scanned them. It made me have to blink several times. After a moment, a light flashed green.

The door opened, and I noticed it was made of dense metal behind the facade of wood. I gasped as Emmerich pushed me inside before anyone noticed us.

It was nicer inside. A lot nicer. The room was lined with machinery, weapons and the occasional appliance. I recognized some but others looked foreign, making me curious. One I swore looked like a 'Timey-wimey detector.' If it went 'ding' I would run out of there.

A guy with ginger hair and wearing a maroon and beige jumpsuit sat on one of the two worn, gray couches occupying a good chunk of the square footage. The couches looked comfy, and a screen hung on the wall which I figured must be some sort of television. It was currently off, but music was coming from the speakers. I recognized the tune, but it was unlike anything I had heard in Portland. It had a soothing atmosphere, yet something about it kept you awake. It would be perfect music to listen to while working.

A corridor led to a few separate rooms, but all the doors were shut so I had no idea what they held. My imagination was running wild, but I figured they were probably bedrooms or the bathroom.

The man got up from one of the couches, "Emmerich, you're back."

When he noticed me, he stopped dead and paled like he had seen a ghost. He pointed at me.

"Great galaxies!" he proclaimed as he jabbed his finger at me once more. "Cousin!"

The man started for me, his arms wide, appearing as if he would embrace me. Even though it seemed like an affectionate gesture, I panicked and hid behind Emmerich, knowing he would protect me from this strange man. I knew he probably didn't mean harm, but when someone you don't know comes barreling over to you, it is sort of scary.

Emmerich held out his arm to stop him from scaring

me any further.

"Angela, what..." he began, his round green eyes wide with bewilderment.

"She remembers nothing," Emmerich answered. I peeked out from behind Emmerich's arm.

He studied Emmerich for a moment, then me. "You don't know who I am?"

I examined him, struggling to recall. He had called me cousin, but the recollections wouldn't appear. Although he seemed familiar, it was like a barrier that I couldn't break down, no matter how hard I tried. I may have not remembered, but something came to me.

"Elwood," I said. "You're... Elwood."

He grinned ear to ear. "Yes, I am."

Emmerich turned to me, shocked. "You remembered someone?"

"I don't remember, the name just popped up in my mind," I rubbed my forehead. "It's as if I'm watching a movie piece by piece, only I'm in the movie." It was frustrating, and hard to handle.

Elwood sat down to take in what we had said.

"Where did you find her? What happened?" Elwood asked, delighted that I was there. It made me feel better he knew me in a positive way. I felt more connected to the area and could believe that I was from here. Maybe I finally discovered my home and I would soon get the answers I needed.

"It's complicated, a lot more than we had formerly assumed," Emmerich brushed his thumb against my hand, taking a second to glance at me, as if some kind of hidden language. I wished I could figure out what that secret language was. "There are some things I need to discuss with you, Elwood."

Elwood raised an eyebrow. "Oh?"

Emmerich eyed me. "Things that Angel can't hear. At least, not yet."

Elwood nodded and rose. Emmerich started for one of the closed doors when I clutched his wrist. "Wait, you promised me an explanation. I want to know what is happening and who I am."

"She really remembers nothing, huh?" Elwood whispered.

Emmerich placed his hands on my shoulders and stared at me with his bright blue eyes. "Remember I said that I would have a physician check you out? That physician is Elwood. Once I am done filling him in, then he can see if it is safe to tell you everything. Wasn't that our deal?"

I gave him a frustrated look. He just smiled. I sighed and waved my hand as if giving him permission to leave. "Fine."

"Stay out here. You're safe here, no one can get in. This place is a lot more secure than it appears. We will be quick."

He was nervous I still didn't trust him, and in some ways, he was right. I had an irrational feeling to trust him, but I needed to understand why he was clearly not telling me everything, which made me trust him less. I also didn't like not being able to place all the fragments together. The more time I spent with him, the more I felt I belonged. Now seeing someone else that I could recognize, I felt even safer.

"Do you need anything? Water, perhaps?" Elwood asked before they went into the hallway.

I nodded. "That would be wonderful, maybe something to eat as well?" My mouth felt dry, and my stomach had been growling for the past half hour.

Elwood went to one wall and pressed a switch. A hidden panel opened up from the wall, exposing a cabinet. He snatched a glass and brought it to a little spout and pushed a button. The glass filled with water.

Pushing another switch, he spoke. "Sandwich." Another panel opened and a sandwich came out of the wall. My mouth dropped. Was it like a fridge? Could you suggest anything from it or was it stocked full of items and drew from the selection? I wanted to ask so many questions but I knew it wasn't the time nor the place.

Elwood handed them to me. I thanked him and watched as they departed down the hallway into one of the rooms. They had gone into the second door to the right. If there was any trouble, which I doubted there would be, I knew where to run.

I sat down on the couch, nearest the door they went into, and twirled the water in my glass. So here I was, on another planet. I could feel my heart beating hard in my chest as I took a sip. Everything was starting to hit me: the men after me, running from the cops on Earth, a whole new world. I sat the water down, not wanting to spill it as my hands began to shake. It was all unbelievable, although it explained some questions I had, but there was still a lot I didn't understand. Taking a deep breath, I tried to calm myself down. I wasn't alone, I had Emmerich, and now Elwood. They would keep me safe and help me remember. I hoped.

I remembered Elwood's name, so that was a sign things would get better, right? Although I wasn't alone, I couldn't help but feel lost. Why did I feel this way now that I have finally found my home? I should be excited but I couldn't help but feel as if I had lost a part of myself back in Portland. Now that the past year was meaningless, I was back in the same position I was a year ago—disconnected from the world and still searching.

Why didn't returning reawaken my memories? I rubbed my face with my hands, wishing that maybe it would jolt back a memory. It didn't, of course. I would just have to wait it out.

I took a bite of the sandwich and was shocked to discover it identical to an Italian sandwich I previously had at a deli. I took another nibble. Yes, it tasted like pepperoni and sweet peppers. There was another taste there but I couldn't put my finger on it. It must have been some plant from this world. I would get to learn all the different types of food again.

The music was still playing, so I closed my eyes and listened, letting it take me away from my thoughts. It was serene and if it wasn't for the fact I had so many things running through my mind, I would have fallen asleep. I would have liked to slip into a dream world. But I couldn't, not when I wanted answers.

No one was watching, so I scarfed the sandwich down in less than a minute and leaned back against the couch. Peering up at the silvery ceiling, I sighed.

I hated waiting, as my therapist Mandy had noted many times. It wasn't my fault that people didn't move as quickly as they should. I shook away her analysis of me. It didn't matter anymore now did it? I wondered if she knew I was missing. The cops did since I had called them. How long would they look for me before they gave up? I hated having people worry, but what could I do now? I was clear across the galaxy. It wasn't like I could just call them up.

I heard the creak of a door. I turned, expecting Emmerich or Elwood, instead a broad dark-bearded man stood in the hallway rubbing his eyes. I froze. Who was he and what do I do? Emmerich and Elwood hadn't mentioned another person being here. Should I hide? I hunched behind the couch but it didn't help. If he glanced over, he could still see me. The man must have been an intruder of some sorts. I scanned around but saw nothing I could defend myself with except for a remote for the TV-thing. I debated if I should run for it or go to Emmerich, but the man was between me and that door. So I stayed still.

He was stout and towering, not someone I would choose to mess with. In fact, he looked a lot like the guys who had attacked me. A scar ran along his right cheek and another around his left eye. I didn't even want to consider what had caused those, or what the other guy must have looked like, if he was indeed alive.

He sauntered past me, mumbling something under his breath. He didn't look like he was awake yet. Going over to the wall where Elwood had obtained food, he jammed his finger at a couple of the buttons. The man neglected to obtain a glass though, and orange liquid spilled onto the floor. Cursing under his breath, he scrambled for a cloth from the nearby counter and threw it on the ground and snatched a cup. Once it was full, he took a sip and turned. He saw me and spat it out.

The man wiped away the drops on his beard. "You! How?"

I stood up, my heart pulsing fast. "I..."

"Where did you come from? How did you get here?" he demanded as he started for me. I backed up, scrambling toward the room where Emmerich and Elwood had gone. Second door on the left.

"I don't know," I shrieked at him, hoping that was a sufficient answer and he would leave me alone. He didn't.

"Come on, we have to go," he tried to grab my arm but I jumped back and screamed.

"Rick!"

Emmerich was out the door into the hallway, gun already drawn and aimed at the man. His face concerned, he evaluated the situation before lowering the gun. He rolled his eyes at the guy. "Isaac, what are you doing?"

Isaac froze for a moment, then smiled. "Emmerich,

you're back. That explains why Angela's here. I had thought I found her myself."

Emmerich placed his hand on me for comfort. "No, I found her. I didn't realize you were here or I would have told her. You scared her." He rubbed my back, trying to soothe me. It didn't work, my heart was racing. "She doesn't remember anything."

I watched relief sweep over Isaac's face. His shoulders relaxed as he let out a breath. He scanned me closer. "She doesn't?"

Emmerich shook his head. "No, I just found her. She knows nothing that happened or how she came to lose her memory."

That could change real easily, I wanted to say. All he needed to do was tell me.

"How?" Isaac asked as he refilled his cup for a second time.

"We don't know," Emmerich turned to me and gave me one of his caring faces. "But Angel, if you don't mind, Elwood will run some tests now."

I glanced over at Elwood. He was grinning. I felt like I recognized that smile and it made me feel like I could trust him. "I don't mind."

"Good, meanwhile I will get you up to speed, Isaac," he glanced down at all the orange liquid on the floor.

"After you clean that up, of course."

Isaac frowned and set his cup down on the table. I watched as he snatched the towel and started cleaning up the spill.

Elwood laughed. "At last, the beast cleans."

He glowered at Elwood. "Come a little closer and say that to my face."

"Sorry, I can't. Doctor duties call," Elwood motioned toward the door. "Come on, Angela, we should perhaps leave these two alone."

I followed him inside the room. It looked like a miniature version of a doctor's office on Earth, but the machinery was unusual, like something from Star Trek. A screen hung on the wall by the metal table, next to instruments I didn't recognize, some different scanners, and a chair. At least I could recognize that.

Elwood gestured to the metal table. "Please take a seat."

I did as he suggested, the coolness of the metal against the skin of my leg making me shudder. Why was it constantly so cold in doctor's offices?

He sat down in his chair and rolled over to me. He snagged one contraption from the counter. "Do you mind taking the coat off? It will interfere with some instruments."

I took the coat off, realizing that I was still in my kitten pajamas. I blushed. "After this can I get a change of clothes? I'm kind of sick of running around in my pajamas."

He snickered as I gave him Emmerich's coat. "Why, what's wrong with kittens? Yes, I have something you can put on. Sadly no kittens, though." He placed a metal band around my upper arm. "I am checking your vitals now. You shouldn't feel a thing."

I watched as various numbers appeared on the screen: blood pressure, temperature, and heart rate. If it was only that simple on Earth. I had been poked and prodded way too many times and was extremely glad it was this simple here. Maybe he didn't even have to use a needle to take blood.

Elwood took the band off and listened to my heart and lungs. I took in deep breaths as he asked. He nodded to himself as he took some notes.

"Everything seems fine." He went to the wall and grabbed a light and shined it in my eyes and ears. "I see nothing out of the ordinary, at least so far. Your vitals seem excellent."

"So you don't know what is wrong with me?"

"No, I still have tests to run, especially with something like amnesia. I just wanted to verify your vitals before doing anything else," he grasped some instrument I didn't recognize, but it reminded me of a spatula with a weird metallic box at the end. "Hold this."

I grabbed it, perplexed. I didn't know what it would do and just hoped it wouldn't hurt.

"It won't hurt you," he chuckled as he saw my face.

"You never know."

"You really recall nothing. Now, tell me," Elwood went on as I held this thing in my palm. "What happens when you recall things? Emmerich said you get headaches?"

I nodded. "Terrible ones. I can hardly think straight but they go away after a while."

"Can you still recall the memories after the headache goes away?" he asked as the spatula-thing's light turned a blue color.

"That's unusual," he whispered.

My eyes widened. One of the worst things to hear was when a doctor said something was unusual. "What is it?"

"I'm not certain yet. I will have to cross-analyze." He smiled. "But don't fret about it, it's probably nothing serious. I will figure it out, I am the best doctor on Cartref."

I raised an eyebrow. "Are you the cockiest too?"

He laughed. "Well, I will tell you that your humor hasn't changed. Something I missed this past year."

How well did he know me? He claimed he was my cousin, I wondered if we grew up together. Or were we the type of cousins that didn't get to see much of each other until after we moved out of our parent's home?

"How close were we?" I asked. "I mean, before all this transpired."

"We were like brother and sister growing up, since neither of us had siblings. I've always been at your side, Angela, and I would never regret that."

His answer brought up further questions in my mind. What did he mean at my side? And why would anyone think he would regret it?

"But back to my question." He took the spatula thing away from my hand. "Do you still recall the memories after the headache?"

"Yes. I can remember pieces, but not much. Some things with Emmerich, your name, when we were walking through the city, I knew the wall hadn't been there before. But other than that, there isn't much."

He rubbed his chin. "Hmm, interesting."

That word. I had heard it so many times that I just wanted to scream. "Please don't say 'interesting', I hate it when people use it when referring to me."

"Sorry. How about intriguing?"

I gave him a look, and he laughed. "I'm just joking

with you." He pulled out another scanner-looking thing. "I will test your blood to make sure your loss of memory isn't drug induced."

"But they already did that—" I started, then remembered what Emmerich had said. No one knew about Earth and he didn't want them to know. Why that was, I still didn't quite understand. Not letting the enemies know about Earth made sense, but they already knew. These people were our friends, at least I thought. Did Emmerich not trust them? Or was he afraid that they wouldn't trust him if they knew the truth? That he was an alien from a different world after all and if this place was anything like Earth, he would be dissected and never see the outside world again.

Elwood noticed as I tried to backtrack. "Who did?"

I stared at the contraption, wondering how it worked. Everything here made me so curious, I wanted to learn it all over again. "I ... Doctors where I was."

He let out a sigh. "Emmerich wouldn't tell me either. I had hoped that you would trust me enough to tell me the truth."

Apparently neither Emmerich nor I had trusted Elwood enough to tell him the secret before they kidnapped me, but one of us had to have told someone because there were other people from this world on Earth. Who did I tell? And what would they do with that information?

"I'm sorry," I said.

He smiled. "It's all right, I'm just delighted to see you."

He moved the scanner back and forth in front of me. I looked at it. "I wish I could say the same."

"You will," he stopped and put the instrument into some sort of machine. "Going through this again, you recall my name, but not anything about me. You remember some things of Emmerich, otherwise I don't think you would come here with him willingly. Or you are way too trusting, which is a possibility, knowing you like I do."

I wished I understood what he meant by that. Was I too trusting in my former life? Had that gotten me into the trouble that I currently was in? "I... I remember feeling comfortable around him, that we were close somehow. That's about it."

"You called him Rick just now. You're the only one who ever called him that, you know."

I shook my head. "I didn't even realize I had. But when I first ran into him, the name appeared in my mind, just like it did yours."

"What about Isaac?"

I shook my head. "No, I didn't recognize him. Still don't."

"You didn't know him as well I guess. He was one of your guards, but you didn't know him that well. As for the people closest to you, that was me, Emmerich and..." he paused. "What do you remember about Michael? Does the name ring any bells?"

"Michael?" I asked. A face flashed in my mind. Serious and stern with dark hair and green eyes. He wore some type of uniform, dark blue. I winced. It felt like someone had stabbed a needle in my brain. "Ow."

Elwood placed his hand on my arm. "Are you all right?"

"I'm fine, but Michael... A dark haired man, am I right? He looked angry in my mind—mad about something or someone. Who is he?"

Elwood stared at me, as if he was about to say something but just shook his head. "I think that's enough, I was afraid this would happen. We have to take it slow, okay? Baby steps."

I nodded, the pain still there, though dulled. I hated this, I hated having to either suffer for my memories or not remember anything at all. I didn't know which was worse.

Opening a drawer, Elwood grabbed a small bottle of a liquid. "Take about 30-60 drops of this once every four hours, it should make the pain go away."

I opened it and it smelled like one of the herbal medicines I took. I sipped it and the headache started to go away. "Thank you."

Elwood stood up. "Come on, we'll get you some new clothes and some water." He took me back into the main room. Emmerich and Isaac sat on one of the couches. The music was off now, but the screen was on, displaying a map. They stopped talking when we entered and Isaac clicked the screen off.

"How did it go?" Emmerich asked.

Elwood patted my back. "Running some tests to figure if there was cause for it, other than that she seems normal. I tried to have her recall some things but when she did, her head started hurting."

Emmerich hurried to my side and clutched my hand. "Are you all right, though?"

Before I could respond, Elwood gave him a look. "She's fine, Romeo. I wouldn't hurt my cousin, now would I? When I have the test results back, we'll have a better idea of what happened."

"What did she remember?" Isaac asked as he joined the line of people. I fidgeted with my sleeves.

"She remembered what Michael looked like when I mentioned his name. That is as far as we got," he turned to the hallway. "I will get her some new clothes.

Something a little more practical."

He must have read my mind. "Thank you," I called after.

Emmerich stepped closer. "Did you remember anything else about Michael other than what he looked like?"

"I don't..." More pain. I grabbed my head.

"I'm sorry, I didn't mean to cause you to get another headache, I thought since you had already remembered..." he began.

I shook my head. "It's fine, I want to remember," I rubbed my forehead.

"What did I just say about asking her questions?" Elwood said as he came back out into the hallway. He handed me a jumpsuit similar to his, but this one was white and orange.

It looked like the perfect size. Was it mine from before?

"No, wait," I said. A dull pain was still there, but it was lessening and images began to appear. "He and I were close, weren't we? I remember you, Rick, and him, standing together. We were discussing something," I paused and looked at him confused as to what else I had seen. "Why do I see mermaids?"

"You remember the water colony?" Emmerich asked, hopeful. "What do you remember about them?"

I shook my head. "Not much, I just I remember an argument about leaving them out of something. Michael wanted to fight, but I said no," I stopped. "What was my job here?"

Emmerich and Elwood exchanged a look. Isaac just stared at me, worried. There was something going on and I felt it was bigger than I could have ever imagined.

Elwood finally spoke. "How about you rest? We don't want you to overwhelm yourself on your first day back, okay?"

"No, I can handle it. Tell me."

"You were an advocator for peace," Emmerich answered before anyone else could. "You stood up for what you believed was right and had a lot of supporters. A born leader."

I nodded. "Okay. Was that so hard?" Although nothing rang a bell, I was happy to get some sort of answer. I couldn't see myself as a leader, though. It didn't sound right.

Elwood snapped his fingers. "I promised you some water," he hurried to the equipment on the wall.

"Way to change the subject," I whispered to Emmerich.

He laughed. "It's amazing how Elwood can ease a tense situation. He is more like a jester than a doctor sometimes, but I think that's what makes him a great doctor. He always knows what to say to cheer you up."

"You think he can fix me?"

Emmerich looked at me and smiled. "If I had to bet on it, I would put all my money on him."

I sighed. "I just hope you're right."

Elwood brought over the glass. "Here."

"Thanks." It helped get rid of the herbal taste that was still in my mouth.

"You should probably get some sleep, Angel," Emmerich said. "You did a lot of running and deserve it. There isn't much for you to do anyway as Elwood goes over the results. If you need anything, we will be in here. Elwood, will you show her to her room?"

Elwood nodded and gestured toward the furthest door down the hallway. I entered it.

It was plain, the only furnishings being a bunk bed and a dresser. There was a door that appeared to lead to a bathroom.

"Sorry it's not that fancy," Elwood teased.

"It's fine, I like it better this way," I smiled, remembering my sparse Portland apartment. "Wake me up when you find out the results, please?"

He nodded. "I will. Just get some rest." With that, he left me in this room. My headache still lingered, though not as strong. Usually it would have gone away by now.

Maybe the herbs weren't as strong as the ones on Earth, though they sure didn't taste that way.

I took a quick shower and changed into the jumpsuit. I was going to go to sleep but I didn't want to wake up and not have time to change again. I wanted to be ready.

The strange thing was, it fit me perfectly. I never found clothes that fit me this perfectly, at least not ones that I could afford. I looked in the mirror. I never thought I could look so good in a jumpsuit.

Letting my tiredness overcome me, I slipped under the covers. I couldn't sleep though I was tired. I tossed and turned, my mind racing. When I did finally manage to fall asleep, I was plagued by nightmares.

I stood, staring down at this strange city Emmerich had brought me to. I was completely alone. I could see everything, from the buildings that no longer looked high, to the wall surrounding the city. Fires raged below, people ran around screaming, completely out of control. I didn't know what to do. I felt helpless as the people panicked.

Beings were coming out of the ocean just beyond the wall. I watched in horror as soldiers on both sides of the wall started firing their weapons, destroying the wall between them. I screamed for them to stop but there was no one to hear me. They attacked it again and again until finally it collapsed into rubble and the two now faced each other.

They charged at one another, weapons aimed and ready. One fired, and all hell broke loose.

War was happening below, people came out of the sea and attacked those on the land, those on the land ready for them to come. Blood stained the streets as both species lay dead. A mountain of bodies began to pile up. No one could stop this madness.

I screamed again and again. But no one heard me. No one listened but went on with their madness. The only way I could stop them was if I got down from the tower.

So I jumped down toward the city. I fell and fell and braced myself as the ground came closer and closer...

As my eyes opened to the real world, my heart felt as if it would leap out of my chest. My head still hurt, pain shooting through it. I moaned and realized that it was all a dream and for that I was glad. I had jumped from hundreds of feet in the air and probably wouldn't have survived. What was I thinking? Why would I do that to stop a war that had nothing to do with me?

A quick glance around reminded me that I was no longer in my apartment. I was on Cartref, a planet in a whole different galaxy than that of Earth. I took a few more deep breaths. I had come here with Emmerich, this was my home. This was where I belonged

Or so I hoped.

Rubbing my eyes, I decided to get up. I didn't want to go back to sleep after that awful dream. I hated dreams where I was falling, my heart always raced when I woke up and I had to calm myself down. I stood up and started to pace around the room.

I had dreamt of this world and of a war. Was it real? What did it have to do with me? I felt like somehow it did. I stopped and bit my lip. Those beings had come out of the ocean on the other side of the wall. Was that why it was there, to stop whatever was on the other side from coming in?

I could hear Emmerich and the others arguing about something, the sound of their voices coming from the crack under the door. I could only make out a few words, but I heard my name more than once. They were arguing about something, something having to do with me.

Maybe I could figure out more of what was going on if I could hear the entire conversation.

Was I going to stoop to that level to figure out what was going on? Listening in on other people's conversation. I didn't want to be that person, but I needed answers. It wasn't my fault they were being so loud. I crept out of the bed and knelt down next the door. I opened it a crack.

"She needs to know the truth now, before it is too late," I heard Emmerich say. "This war could erupt any moment now."

So there was a war. I was right.

"I already told you, giving her information could affect her mind. The results from the tests aren't clear, whatever it is in her system, I haven't seen before. As a medic I can't allow you to tell her anything," Elwood answered.

I gulped. That wasn't something I wanted to hear. Not when Emmerich said Elwood was one of the best doctors around. Who else could help me?

"But what about as her family? What do you say then? We can't just keep her in the dark, we need her." Emmerich went on.

There was a long pause.

"I have to go with Elwood on this one," Isaac said. "We can't risk hurting her."

Isaac... he still wasn't triggering any memories. It unnerved me that I couldn't remember who he was. At least with the others I remembered something, even if it was just a feeling. With Isaac I felt... nothing.

"She has some sort of poison in her blood," Elwood went on, "It's what is causing her mind to block out memories and cause her pain. We have to figure out how to get it out of her system before we do anything. I will not risk her life without knowing more."

Poison? I wondered how long it had been in my body and whether he could get rid of it. I bit my thumb. Why did this happen to me? Who poisoned me to wipe clean my memories?

"But we can't just keep everything from her," Emmerich yelled, frustrated as I was. "She needs to know who she is, the war, and everything that Michael has done. Before it is too late."

I grabbed my head as it started hurting again. That name. I was having a conversation with Michael. I wanted peace, I wanted a treaty. Michael was furious. He wanted war, saying that the Galaftns were no match for us. They were the weaker species, and we had to put them in their place. Our argument got very heated and Emmerich came into the room, asking what was going on.

I blinked, the images faded, but the headache didn't. I rubbed my forehead, hoping that would help, but it didn't. One question kept running through my mind: Who were Galaftns?

Done with eavesdropping, I stepped out to where they were discussing me. I had to stand up for myself. I couldn't let them decide for me.

They stared at me, looking surprised to find me awake.

They were probably hoping I hadn't heard them talking about me, but I had. And now I wanted answers, especially about Michael and the Galaftns.

Emmerich was the first to break the silence. "Angel, I thought you were asleep."

"I couldn't sleep, I heard you three," I rubbed my head, the pain still lingering from the recalled memories. "I just..."

"Did you remember something else?" Elwood asked, worried.

I ignored his question. "What are Galaftns?"

Emmerich looked at Isaac and Elwood. "What did you remember? How much of our conversation did you hear?"

I fidgeted with the sleeve of my jumpsuit. Not only did it fit me, the edge I was fidgeting with was already worn. "It came to me just now when I heard you discussing Michael. I remember arguing about it with him. Something about a war. Who or what are they?"

No one said a word.

I felt my blood heat up—the pressure of the last few days coming to a boil. "Tell me the truth Rick! Someone, please!"

"If I do that," Emmerich whispered. "I could hurt you. I can't do that to you, Angel, if anything happened..."

I shook my head and ran my fingers through my hair in frustration. My head was pounding now. "But I heard you just now, you said you couldn't keep me in the dark like this."

"I won't let him," Elwood added. "You have poison in your system and I don't know what will happen."

"Why don't you let me make that decision? It's my life, not yours. I can live with the consequences."

"If that means your death, I could never live with myself. I'd rather die than let any harm like that come to you," Elwood replied.

"Why? Why do I mean so much to you, to any of you? Do you have any idea what it's like not knowing who you are, or who anyone else is?" I took a breath, willing myself to calm down. "I want to understand, I want to help."

"In due time," Emmerich whispered as he wrapped his arms around me. "Let us figure it out."

I shook my head. "No, I have to know now. Who was I? Why am I so important?"

"Angel, just..."

My head was pounding and I couldn't think straight. I wanted it all to go away. I shoved past him and headed toward the entry door. "If you won't tell me anything. I'll go find my own answers."

"No, don't go out there!" he tried to grab me, but I shoved him back.

"Leave me alone if you aren't going to help me," my voice was dark, it sounded strange even to me. I had had enough with everything.

"But there are people—" he began.

I threw my hands up. "What people? I'm not hearing any explanations."

"Listen to your cousin, we don't know what it could do to you," Isaac added.

"You're treating me like a child, all of you. Don't you see that? Leaving me in the dark, discussing what to do about me instead of just asking? Do you have any idea how that makes me feel? Everyone for the past year has treated me the exact way you are now. I am not putting up with it anymore," I started to open the door. Elwood and Isaac didn't try to follow. It was as if they knew it was up to Emmerich and somehow I understood. He was the only one who could calm me down, except at this point I didn't want to.

"You have nowhere to go! It's not safe," Emmerich yelled as I started down the street.

I turned around to face him. "How would I know that? How can I know what is safe and what isn't if you don't tell me! Who should I be afraid of? I can't fight if I don't know."

Emmerich ran after me. "I won't let you!"

I shook my head and turned my back to him. "I must have been one hell of a little princess if I always let someone else deal with my problems."

"Angel! Wait! Please!"

"I need to get some fresh air. Leave me alone."

He snatched my wrist and pulled me back. "No, you aren't going out there alone."

I looked him in the eyes. "What does it matter to you, huh? What am I to you?"

His face was red. I had gotten under his skin. Maybe he would realize I was right. "Stop acting like I am the bad guy! I'm trying to help you!"

"From whom? From what? The big bad wolf? The unseen enemy that I apparently have?" I shouted back.

"I saved you from those men back at your apartment, isn't that enough?"

I frowned. "So what, you are my knight in shining armor? I should just follow you everywhere?"

He took a deep breath and let it out slowly. He glanced around, worried. "Please stop, you are making a scene. Someone might notice you."

"Oh really?" I turned to a person walking past and pulled their sleeve to get their attention. I held out my hand. "Hello there, I'm Angela Starr. And what's your name?"

I expected the person just to look at me like I was some kind of nut and then go on with her day. Instead the woman stared at me with her aged eyes, her wrinkled mouth opened. She looked as if she had seen a ghost. I was speechless. I didn't think she would recognize me. I glanced at Emmerich and he was wide-eyed, worried. The woman hurried away, pulling a child with her. I watched as she ran off.

I pointed at her. "Why... why did she do that?" I looked at Emmerich, who had a stern look on his face. "Did she recognize me? That's not possible. How..."

Emmerich placed his hand on my back. "Angel, please come with me. I promise to tell you everything."

I shook my head and pushed his hand away. My head still hurt, pounding, making everything spin. I just wanted answers, and I wanted nothing else. The pain hurt so bad. "No, you tell me right now. Who was I?"

He grabbed my arm and started to drag me.

"Let me go!" I shouted, pulling out of his grasp. I should have just gone with him, but my head was pounding and I couldn't think straight. So I started running. I didn't know where or why, I just wanted to get away from it all: the pain, the confusion, the lies. I wanted all of it to disappear and the harder I ran, the more I felt like I could.

"Angel, don't!" Emmerich yelled.

I ignored him as he tried to follow. I zigzagged through the streets. I could get through the small gaps between people that Emmerich could not. I could hear people shouting as he shoved past them. I hoped they would slow him down so I could just get away from it all. I needed a break from everything; at least that is what the pain in my head was telling me.

I was still in the run-down area, but there were more people, and the towering wall was still not too far in the distance. The streets stunk of sweat and blood but I didn't care. I kept on running, with Emmerich not too far behind. He should give up, it would be easier if he just gave up and I could walk around in peace and escape all of this nonsense.

As I bumped into people, they stared at me, mouths wide and fingers pointing. They recognized me. My heart quickened, beating faster than I could keep up. Why did they recognize me? How could all these people know me? I felt like Alice in Wonderland as all the eyes were looking at me. Stop it, I wanted to shout. Just stop it. I tried to ignore them but as more and more turned to stare, I began to worry.

And I didn't know why.

My head pulsed as I kept racing forward. Everything was so confusing, just a jumbled mess. I should just stop, I knew, and let Emmerich take me back, but something in the back of my mind demanded I run, telling me the pain would stop if I could just get away. Was it the poison working, because just a few hours ago I wouldn't have dreamed of running from Emmerich, the one person I thought I could trust. The poison was controlling me, now I knew. And I couldn't do anything about it.

The world felt like it was spinning around me and I was about to lose control. I tried to steady my breathing, but everything felt rushed and I couldn't do anything about it. Sweat began to pour off my skin and my vision was becoming blurry. My stomach hurt and every muscle in my body began to burn. So this is what it felt like to be poisoned. This couldn't get any worse.

That thought was completely and utterly wrong.

As I turned around another corner, I felt a hand grab my wrist.

I spun around to tell Emmerich off. I wanted to be alone, at least I thought I did. "Rick, I told you—"

It wasn't Rick. And now I wished it was. Instead the man that had my wrist was a tall, muscular man with a large brown mustache and bald head. I screamed.

Two other men came and helped him subdue me, all wearing dark blue uniforms, similar to the one I had remembered Michael wearing. On the arm of each uniform was a cross with two X's underneath.

"Rick!" I yelled as one pulled me toward a hover craft like I had seen earlier, except this one had windows tinted black and the symbol from their uniforms was on the side. I tried to kick and flail, but it didn't help. The three brutes forced me into the craft. I could see Emmerich rounding the corner and pulling out his gun as he sprinted for the craft. I was hopeful for a moment, but realized it was too late.

The door slammed shut and I could see Emmerich no longer.

The men didn't say a word as the machine moved through the city. I couldn't see out of the windows in the back, but I could feel as we flew around. It made me nauseous, on top of the sweat that poured off my skin. I could hardly breathe and I didn't know if it was from their flying or if something else was happening. My head still pounded, pain jolting through my entire body. I tried to not think about it as I fidgeted with my necklace, keeping hope that Emmerich would come for me.

I asked my captors again and again where they were

taking me. They didn't answer, but told me to stop talking. I finally did, not wanting them to shoot me as they threatened to do. No one here ever told me anything. I shouldn't have even tried.

I felt like crying but I was stronger than that. I had to keep my composure.

The pain shooting through my body took all my willpower to stay conscious. I didn't want to pass out. I had to figure out who was kidnapping me and what they wanted. I had to stay strong, even though the poison that Elwood found was coursing through my blood. Why it had triggered now, I had no idea. Could it have been from some memories? I just hoped Elwood would figure it out and that I wouldn't have to suffer much longer.

I tried not to think about Rick. All this was my fault. Was he worried about me? Or was he mad that I had caused all of this? I wanted to go back and apologize. I hoped he had some new ingenious way of saving me, after all, he had made it all the way across the galaxy to save me once before. How was this any different? I sure didn't know what to do, I was on a planet in a different galaxy, I had no clue what to do.

But did I need saving?

That was the question, wasn't it? I tried to go through every scenario in my head. Maybe the person who captured me just wanted to talk. Or maybe they wanted me dead since the men in Portland had weapons and were ready to kill me. I hoped these weren't the same people who had tried to kill me before, but I felt they were. Taking deep breaths, I tried not to panic. I would make it out fine, I had so far.

Emmerich said many had thought me dead, but he knew I was still alive. These people knew. These men were taking me somewhere, so they didn't want to kill me yet. I would get answers, in the end.

Before they tried to kill me.

After a while, we decelerated and landed. The men climbed out of the craft and pulled me out. I stumbled, not able to keep my balance by myself.

It was bright, the system's star shining down on the planet along with the reflection off of the two giant moons. It took a moment for my eyes to adjust to the light and when I did, I couldn't believe what I saw.

"What the hell?" I breathed. "Where are we?"

It had to be a palace for some sort of royalty. Nothing I had seen on Earth could compare to the grandeur of this place. I gaped at the opulent fifty-story building. Dark green vines blooming with purple flowers wove along the stones and trailed down the mountain, with the rest of the city laid out far below us. Sculptures of beasts and people lined the walls. Magnificent didn't even describe it.

"Move!" One of the men yelled, pushing me forward. I almost fell and the other guard pulled me back up and dragged me into the palace. My legs felt like jelly and I could barely steady them. What was wrong with me?

The inside was spectacular, covered with carvings of flying creatures, like dragons, with serpent scales covering their bodies and their wings spread fifty feet across. Even though it was all white, I could imagine their colors being vibrant purples, greens, and blues, shimmering if they were in the light. Their wings were larger than life. Their beauty surpassed that of any animal I had ever seen.

There were also carvings of four-legged creatures with large manes which appeared to breath fire. A group was sculpted attacking a large bird-like animal that fought back with water. The detail was spectacular, it looked like the waves were moving. Maybe they were, for all I knew.

Additional small beasts were carved around them, fighting alongside their masters. The little ones looked like miniatures of their masters and were just as ferocious. The carvings were so thorough, I could almost pretend they were real.

It was magnificent.

I wondered if the creatures were real or mythical. I had

seen things similar to them on Earth, but they were all made up in someone's mind. This place might have these beings. It wouldn't have surprised me if they were real, not after seeing the dragon in that one shop. This place reminded me of pictures I had seen of ancient Rome or Greece in textbooks, back when they were thriving empires and not just ruins.

Everyone stared at me as the guards marched me through the hall. I tried to ignore them but I couldn't. I wanted to know how they knew me, why they stared. They all wore uniforms like those of my captors.

We came to a halt in front of a door which swooshed open. Yes, swooshed, like on a sci-fi show. My captors shoved me inside and pushed a button on the wall and I felt the room move underneath my feet. An elevator.

Only it didn't just move up and down. I tried not to fall over as we also moved side to side. My captors didn't budge with the changes in acceleration.

We finally stopped, and the door slid open to reveal quite a different setting. Instead of bright white stone, the walls were painted a dark blue. Dim lights filled the hallway, and shadows danced across the floor as we made our way down the hallway.

We passed only a few doors as we moved down the hallway, all closed. It felt familiar, as if I had been here before, only I didn't feel it should be this dark or uninviting. I remembered it being lighter, warmer. I wanted people to feel welcome, not turn them away.

I did?

My head started to pound yet again. That was all I needed, for the headache to get worse. I didn't think that was possible until I felt yet another jolt stab through my mind. I focused on fighting it, frustrated with having to deal with this on top of whatever would happen in this palace, whether or not my captors were going to kill me.

Was it ever going to stop?

We finally came to a halt in front of a door and one soldier slid a key card into a slot and then stepped in front of a scanner similar to the one Emmerich had, and it read his eye. A couple of moments later, the light turned green, and the door opened. They shoved me inside and closed the door, leaving me alone to wait.

I stumbled and fell to the floor, scraping my hands on the rough stone. The jerks didn't need to shove me, I would have gone in if they had just asked.

I got up and examined my hands. The skin wasn't cut, but they still stung. I straightened my jumpsuit as I looked around the room.

The walls were painted blue like the hallway; a color like that of the sky on a crisp winter's eve, lined with a light beige close to the color of the stone used to carve the mystical creatures. A large desk took up part of the room, although the room was so large, the desk looked like a toy in comparison. A fireplace was on the opposite side of the desk, a fire currently blazing within. Despite that, the room was cold.

Paintings of battle scenes hung above the fireplace. There were eight, based on the changes in clothing, I assumed they were all from different points in history. I stared at them. They hadn't hung there before, but I recognized them from somewhere. More pain shot through my head.

The wars of centuries past.

One stood out from the rest. I studied it as I fiddled with my necklace. The battle scene took place in a forest, the water bird from the sculptures in the lobby flew above. The fire creature was there too, maybe it symbolized the fight between good and evil. Men in either white and orange uniforms or dark green robes lay dead on the forest floor. In the middle stood a man. His hair was ginger and eyes blue as the sea. He held up a sword in victory. I stared at the eyes, wondering. Who was he and why did he seem so familiar?

I gave up trying to recall the memory. I stroked the mantle. The same bird-like creatures were etched into the marble, a stream of water connected them. It was spectacular. If I wasn't worried someone would come in, I might have enjoyed it.

Large glass windows took up the other wall. I could see the entire city below. The buildings were a lot lower compared to this palace, just like in my dream. I could see everything that surrounded the palace, even the glistening water beyond the walls. So it was an ocean, I was right.

Mermaids. I couldn't believe there were such creatures, but I reminded myself where I was— anything was possible.

I watched as several crafts flew through the city. Everyone had things to do, places to be, and here I was. Kidnapped, probably waiting to be executed.

And none of them would ever know.

It was scary to think how that was possible, how it wouldn't matter to any of them if I lived or died. No one would notice. None except for Emmerich, Elwood and Isaac. It was crazy to think that, but it was true. I should have stayed with them, none of this would have happened if I had.

Usually they went away after the memory came, or at least a few minutes later. This one had been building up since before I went to sleep. Why wasn't it going away?

Did it have to do something with the poison?

I saw one of the flying aircrafts out in the distance, moving higher than the rest. It didn't seem to be following the flow of traffic.

Before I could see what it would do, the door to the room opened behind me. I turned to find a man with dark hair, wearing a well-tailored suit. A smirk was on his face as he strolled over to where I stood.

"Who are you?" I asked, backing away toward the glass. I knew there was nowhere for me to go, but I wanted to be as far away from him as possible.

He stopped. "What did you just say?"

"I asked you who you were," I repeated although in that instant, I knew him. He was Michael, but yet he wasn't. Something seemed different from my memories.

This man was more menacing. That's what it was. And cocky.

He laughed. "Does our dear Angela Starr not remember me?"

I shook my head. "I don't remember anything. I woke up a year ago with no memory. What's going on?"

"Well, well, this changes things, doesn't it?" He grabbed me by the jaw and traced my chin with his thumb. I let out a squeak, half expecting him to hurt me. Surprisingly, he didn't. "The poison worked, just not as planned. Maybe I won't need to kill you."

I pulled away. "You did this? Why?"

"Because you were the one thing that stood in the way of all of this," he motioned around. "You and Emmerich."

"What are you talking about, I don't know..."

He looked at me, grinning. "He didn't tell you the truth? Hmm, this is interesting indeed, your lover not giving you all the information."

Did he just say lover? What was he talking about? "My what? Who are you?"

He bowed. "I am Michael Dansolf, once her majesty the Empress of Cartref's second in command." He looked up at me, his gaze meeting mine. "Once your second in command."

"My... what?" Pain engulfed everything. The coronation, the crown, everything was coming back. I grabbed my throbbing head and knelt down. "No, that's impossible! I can't be—"

"You aren't. Not anymore. Because I had you assassinated," he said and shrugged. "Or at least I tried. I used a Galaftn poison, so they would be blamed and the war could start. Although you didn't die, it did work. All your people hate them and want them to be destroyed."

I remembered. It had felt like acid in my body, the poison. Just like it did now. Someone had needed to hold me down. "You tried to kill me? Why?"

He knelt down next to me. "Isn't it obvious? I wanted what you had. And you never listened, you had these ideas of equality and peace between the Galaftns, all from your stupid lover," he made a gagging noise as he stood up and paced the office. "Pathetic. They didn't deserve it. So I did something about it."

The memories flashed through my mind, faster and faster. The Galaftns, the mermaids. That's who I kept seeing in my visions, the Galaftns. They were the people from the water. I remembered now, we were talking peace. There was a treaty to be signed. I didn't want war, not then, not ever. It wasn't me, I enjoyed discussing options and coming to an agreement. I wasn't like the Emperors before me, I wasn't like my father, and his father before him. I hated letting my people die for what I thought was no good reason. I had vowed to never be like them. I would keep that promise.

The poison was taking over my body. Maybe it wouldn't matter now, I would probably die. After everything, this was how I would die. Typical, I had never been lucky, starting with being born in this blood-lusting family, then having to take the crown at such a young age. It was coming back to me, all of it.

And Emmerich, I remembered the day I found him.

The only luck in my life.

But Michael had said lover. That couldn't be right, could it?

"What did you say about..." The pain was overwhelming, and I gasped.

"What's going on with you?" Michael asked as he looked down at my misery. He seemed to enjoy it.

I glared up at him, as if he didn't know. "With every recovered memory comes pain. Something to do with that poison you gave me. Seems to have never left my system."

He laughed, enlightened by the news I had told him. "Well, this is quite the development. That's why he hasn't told you everything, isn't it? So you wouldn't be in pain," he bent down to my level and whispered into my ear. "I will just have to be the one to fill in the gaps then, won't I? That boy appeared a few years back, out of nowhere, in the palace. We would have executed him for trespassing and not having an identification chip, but you decided to talk to him instead. Next thing I knew you were sleeping with him, because I guess that's what you do with foreigners," he seemed almost... jealous. "You never told me where he came from, every time, you ignored the question and said it wasn't important. But I had to figure it out myself, what kind of second in command would I have been if I didn't know who my boss was in bed with," he paused, licking his lips. "Then I figured it out. He was from, a different planet. Who would have thought.?

"It was you, you figured out where it was and sent me there. How?"

He chuckled. "I had you two watched. Listened as he talked about a faraway land. There wasn't much about you two that I didn't find out. He tried to understand how he did it, you know, writing notes. I had my men solve it and, well, you know the rest." He stood up and walked around his desk. "He filled you with ideas of peace and humanism, and all that crap, so you decided instead of raging war against the Galaftns, to make peace. I couldn't let that happen, I just couldn't."

I shook my head. "Why? Why does it matter to you? Wouldn't you rather have peace?"

He slammed his fists on his desk. "Because they are the enemy! They have always been the enemy! Because of one boy you debased our kind! It was too much, I couldn't let you rule."

"You're insane."

"Serving you made me this way," he said cold-heartedly.

"I trusted you!" I shouted. For an instant I remembered,

I remembered all the things we had done, side by side. "We grew up together. You were my best friend!"

"How time changes, huh? Did your parents ever tell you how my family came to be your second in command? It was because of that war!" He jabbed his finger at the painting I had studied earlier, the one with the man with ginger hair. "That is your great-grandfather pillaging my family's land. We used to have a province on the other side of Cartref, until he came and conquered it all. My family tried to fight, but they were outnumbered. They had no choice but to agree to a treaty, and after years of complete obedience, your great-grandfather made my great-grandfather his second in command. And since then, we all have served at your family's side. It was the only way to survive and not be killed for living our lives away from your family's rule."

I stared at the painting. That was my great-grandfather? It was starting to all come back, along with more pain. I winced. "But he isn't me."

"No, he wasn't. He would have conquered the Galaftns. That is why you are at my mercy, just as it always should have been."

"Then wouldn't you want peace with the Galaftns?" I asked. It made little sense. "Why would you want to do to them what my great-grandfather did to your people?"

"Because they don't deserve peace! If my people couldn't survive, neither should they," he explained.

"You will kill innocent people because you think it will amend the past? You are wrong, these people shouldn't suffer just because your family did. We can finally make amends, we can finally create a world of peace!" I exclaimed.

He let out a brief sigh. "Don't you see, Angela, that isn't possible. Peace just isn't possible in this world and I will not be on the losing side again. I took control, just like it should have been. My family should have won the war, not yours."

"I will give you anything you want, Michael," I begged. "Please, just let me live. Get me to a doctor and we can work this all out. Your people can go back to the province and I promise you peace..."

"Lies!" he shouted, making me jump. "Your great-grandfather also promised us peace if we submitted. Instead, our people were practically made into slaves. We aren't suffering like that again. No, you have to die. You must suffer for what they did."

I shook my head, not believing what he was saying. He was blaming me for something that happened before I was even born. It wasn't fair. "How could you do this to me? We have been together for so many years. You know

I'm not like them."

"It's easy, really." He pulled out a gun and pointed it at me. My heart felt like it had stopped in my chest. He was going to kill me this time, and there was nothing to stop him. "Just like this."

There was no way out of this, I knew. I was a dead woman. All my questions had been answered, and I was going to die. I could never apologize to Rick, I wouldn't see my cousin again. It was over, and Michael had won. There was no way I could beat him, not in my condition. I could barely move.

Rick had risked everything for me and I had repaid him by running into the enemy's hands. I felt like such a fool. My head hurt so much and I was confused and didn't know what I was doing. Everything was a swirling mess and I couldn't make it stop. Now it would end and I wouldn't have to suffer any longer. That was one good thing, I supposed. But I wasn't ready to die, I didn't want Michael to win. I didn't want to make my people suffer because I had failed them. I didn't want to make Emmerich suffer because he had risked so much to bring me back. Because not only was I the true ruler over this place, but he also loved me.

And I loved him.

"Goodbye Angela." The sweet way Michael said it

made me cringe. "It was great seeing you one last time, even though you don't quite remember me. I will try to return the favor and forget all about you."

I closed my eyes, ready for the end. I didn't want to see it coming, I didn't want to face it. Maybe I was a coward, and that was how I had gotten in this mess. I didn't want to start a war. Did that make me a coward? No, that made me a person who always looked for another way. Someone who never gave up trying.

Instead of the sound of a shot being fired, I heard a door slam open, hitting the wall and splintering.

"What the?!" Michael yelled. I opened my eyes to find Emmerich pointing a gun at him. He had found me. He had saved me yet again.

"Let her go, Michael," Emmerich demanded. "No one has to die today."

Michael moved his gun away from me, shaking his head. "How do you do it? How do you always manage to interfere with my plans? Why can't you just go back to where you belong!"

Emmerich made his way over to me. "See, that's what you don't understand. I am where I belong, Michael. I belong at Angel's side."

"No, you both belong in a grave. You are the one who put false ideas of peace and prosperity in her head, made her think she could rule this land without war. You made her into the coward she is," Michael spat. "It is despicable."

"War has brought nothing but pain, you of all people should know that," Emmerich knelt down beside me. "Are you okay?"

I shook my head. "No, the poison is spreading. I can barely move."

"It's too late," Michael laughed. "The poison is no longer dormant in her body. She will be dead soon enough and I won't have to worry about you ruining my plans. I will have won."

"Angel, let's go!" Emmerich grabbed my hand. I heard shots coming from the hallway as guards flooded into the room. They moved toward us with guns raised.

Emmerich pulled me toward the windows and aimed at the window with his gun. He couldn't be serious—did he think we could jump out the window?

"Aren't we hundreds of feet up in the air?!" I yelled as Emmerich shot out the window. Glass shattered in every direction. I blocked the shards from hitting my face.

"Makes it even more fun to jump!"

He pulled me out the window and into the open air. I screamed as he wrapped his arms around me and we tumbled down. I hit something hard. But not as hard as it should have been if we had hit the ground. I opened my eyes to find Elwood standing over me.

"Hey beautiful, did you miss us?" he smiled. He really tried to lighten up every situation, didn't he?

I didn't respond, but glanced around to find myself in the vehicle I had seen earlier. The one I had seen not flowing with traffic, before Michael walked in and tried to kill me after our little chat. Isaac was flying the craft. All three of them had come to rescue me. Man, Rick worked quickly. Good thing he did or I would have been dead. As it was, it was a little too close for comfort.

"What... what?" I began as I tried to stand up, shaking. I didn't quite make it, but collapsed onto the floor. Elwood hurried to my side.

"Are you all right? What's wrong? Did Michael hurt you?"

I didn't answer. I had almost died. Again. It was a lot to take in, especially after jumping out of a window. Maybe Elwood was right, I was way too trusting of Emmerich. We had jumped through a window.

"Poison. It's not dormant anymore."

Elwood's eyes widened. "What? What happened?"

"Love to explain but we have to get out of here before he sends his men after us," Emmerich pushed a button closing the door of the hovercraft. Elwood still knelt next to me, feeling my wrist for my pulse.

"Your pulse is fast. Emmerich, we have to get her out of here!" Elwood called.

"I'm on it!" He sat down at the controls and pushed the craft forward. "Hopefully we can, before..."

The aircraft shook.

"Too late," Isaac said.

I glanced out the back window to find a dozen vehicles following us. All dark with the palace's symbol on them. I took a deep breath, thinking there was no way out of this. I watched lasers come flashing out from each of the craft. Our craft shook again. Crap.

"Emmerich, what are we going to do?" I asked in a panic. I started coughing uncontrollably. Why did I never get a moment to catch my breath, even after almost dying?

"Elwood, help her into a seat! You both need to strap in for what we'll do next," Emmerich called back.

I felt Elwood help me into a seat. I was dizzy, barely able to focus on what was going on around me. This poison stuff sucked. I promised myself that if I survived, I wouldn't ever let myself be poisoned again. That was doable, right?

They strapped me in and Elwood buckled himself in. He whispered something under his breath and shut his eyes. I wondered for a moment why he did that but before I knew it, we went into a wild series of barrel rolls. I clutched the straps, afraid that I would fall out. I shut my eyes tight as we twirled around and around. There was that nauseous feeling again, the one that hadn't gone away from the last time I flew in a craft. I was too weak to throw up though, that was one plus in all this mess.

On top of everything, my head still ached, sweat still poured off my head, and I felt as if I was going pass out at any moment. Memories were coming back in a rush. My mother, my father before they were killed in an accident when I was five. Generations and generations of my family ruling the planet, going to war with any other civilization they found. Colonizing the moons, colonizing another planet in the system. I couldn't believe it, I was the daughter of all this war, all this blood. I didn't want any of it and when they died, I thought I wouldn't have to face that death. Years later, I became the Empress of Cartref, after much training, of course. Many of my family's servants and top commanders helped. Including Michael, who was always at my side.

He was my best friend growing up, always there for me. How could he betray me like that? How could he just decide one day that he would kill me and take my spot as ruler of this planet?

Elwood should have been next in line for the throne, not Michael, but he was a rebel like Emmerich. I wonder what Michael did to take the throne, how he got the people to turn against the royal line without having to kill Elwood. Maybe he had tried to kill him and Elwood got away with Emmerich. There was so much I had missed in the last year and I wanted to put the pieces together. I tried to think it all through but the pain kept building up.

It was what I had wanted, though, wasn't it? The memories to come back, no matter the pain. I regretted ever thinking that, the pain was too much to bear. I wasn't even sure I would survive it all, this poison and the craft attacking us.

Our craft rolled again and again. I kept my eyes shut, not wanting to see the world spin around us. Suddenly we dropped and flew down low, into the city. I opened my eyes to find buildings swishing by.

"Stay away from the pedestrians!" I shouted at Emmerich. I didn't want anyone to get hurt, not if I could help it.

I heard Emmerich mumble something as he brought us back up into the sky. I understood why he wanted to fly low, trying to lose them in the traffic and the maze of buildings. But if something happened to a bystander, I would never forgive myself. That just wasn't my way.

We flew up again. I could see the wall surrounding the city just ahead. We were almost out of the city and above the ocean. Shots hit us again, shaking the entire craft, and I could hear alarms coming from the cockpit.

I glanced at Elwood, he had his eyes shut and was whispering some kind of prayer under his breath. That was not reassuring. I looked up at the cockpit and swallowed down the bile. "Is everything all right in there?" I shouted at the cockpit.

"Fine and dandy!" Emmerich answered. "Might explode at any second, other than that fine!"

"I would really appreciate it if you fixed that!" I said back.

"All right, will do my best!"

The craft shook again, and I was sure that we were done for. The beeps from the cockpit were getting louder and now there were red flashing lights, too. I could feel the craft shuddering and not wanting to stay in the sky.

Why could nothing ever be easy?

Then it stopped. No more shots were being fired at us and the lights and beeping stopped. The ride started to smooth out, and I glanced back to find the vehicles following us had turned around and left. I blinked a couple of times, half expecting it to just be my imagination. No, they were turning around.

Had they just given up? No, it couldn't be that simple. I waited for them to reappear and destroy us once and for all, but they were gone for good.

Wanting to get a better look, I unbuckled my straps and stood up. That was stupid of me. Everything went blurry, and I collapsed back to the ground.

"Angel!" Emmerich rushed to my side. I watched as Elwood unbuckled and grabbed a med kit. "Stay awake, please."

"My head, too much," I gasped as I started to lose my vision. After all that, was this really the way I would go? No, I wouldn't allow it. I had to overcome this, especially after everything I had gone through in these past few days.

But the pain was overwhelming.

Everything became a jumble as I heard Emmerich and Elwood shouting. I felt someone pull me back up onto the seat. Fingers forced my eyes open and I could see a bright light.

"The poison," I heard Elwood say. "Michael must have known it was going through her system. That's why they gave up on us. He knew there was no reason to come after us."

"Please tell me you have a cure," Emmerich said as I felt him stroke my hand.

"Not on me, no. We have to get her to a facility, we have to figure out what they gave to her," Elwood explained as he rummaged through the med kit.

"Galaftns," I murmured. "Michael said it was from..." I started to lose consciousness.

"No, no, don't you dare lose consciousness on me cousin! Don't you dare!" Elwood slapped my face a few times, but it was no use. My body had given up.

I collapsed into Emmerich's arms.

Free

Defeat the enemy and take their land. Don't let anyone destroy what was ours. That was what I had been taught from day one. Show no mercy and don't give in. I was to be ruthless, never letting emotion sway me. Straight-faced, I should never look back.

Those were the lessons my parents hammered into me every day until their death. I could remember now—everything they had said, every moment. I even recalled the tales of war grandfather had told before he passed away so long ago. It had been a gruesome war: all the blood spilt, the destruction of the Goedwig, native beings of the forest. They looked just like us in every way, humans, but grandfather insisted that they were offspring of the devil himself.

I had been trained to be a fearless leader, but there was only one problem: I was afraid.

Every night I fell asleep afraid for the day to come. I didn't want war and hate; I wanted to live in peace. I saw the people I ruled as my friends, and I wanted to treat any other beings on the planet, or on another planet, the same way. But that wasn't the way of my ancestors. They were power-hungry and wanted to rule the land with an iron fist. Most times I cried myself to sleep.

Then my parents died, along with my aunt and uncle who would have ruled in my stead until I was seventeen. I didn't know what to do; I was a lost little girl. Michael had helped me get back on my feet and taught me everything else I needed to do, how to act, what was wanted of me. But through it all I knew none of it was me. I wasn't a leader, at least not the power-hungry one my people wanted. I stood for peace, not war.

Then one day, a man appeared out of nowhere. He called himself Emmerich and after a while; I found out his secret—he was from a completely different world. He understood my fears and told me about how war on his own Earth had devastated millions. Many were homeless, abandoned, orphaned, in pain, lost... I couldn't let my people suffer like that. I promised myself I never would.

Not long after that, the Galaftns appeared from out of the oceans, wanting peace. My people begged to go to war, and, more importantly, so did Michael. I wouldn't hear of it. We began a long-running argument. Working behind my back, he organized riots. I found him out, but then he poisoned me. Chaos filled the streets. Michael was doing a perfect job of getting my people to turn on me. There was so much pressure to declare war, it was a wonder that I could even get a wink of sleep at night. But Emmerich stayed by my side to make sure I wouldn't waiver. I don't know what I would have done if he hadn't shown up—or where I would be today. I probably would have caved in to the pressure, or worse, be dead.

Even with his help, though, too much weight was on my shoulders. The people met any group of Galaftn who entered the city with violence and it took everything I had to speak to them without incident. It surprised me that they kept seeking peace after everything they had endured with my people.

Days and nights went by and my people became more violent. I was having horrible nightmares about my people torturing them in the streets, and that I had finally given in and declared war.

The same nightmares I was having right now.

Hands were reaching for me, wanting to drag me down with them as they returned into oblivion. Countless destroyed souls, all wanting my blood. They clawed at me, leaving scratches down my arms and legs. I screamed for help, but there was no one there to help me, only darkness wanting to rip me apart. I tried to run but I couldn't move. I was surrounded.

And it was all my fault.

I had sent them to fight; I had declared war when I didn't have to. They were exacting their revenge because I was weak and had caused them to lose their lives. I wasn't my father; I wasn't my grandfather. I was a young girl who wanted peace instead of war. I was a girl who believed in good and wanted to live in a world where there was no suffering and fighting. Was that just too much to ask?

"Angel, take my hand!" a voice called from the darkness.

It was Emmerich. I could hear him but I couldn't find him. "Emmerich, help!"

"Take my hand!"

I searched and searched but I couldn't find his hand— there were too many grabbing me. Tears ran down my face. I couldn't hold on any longer, they were pulling me down.

"Emmerich!"

I opened my eyes to find it had all been a dream. Rubbing my head, everything was coming back to me in one big rush. My parents. My grandfather. The thirst of war. The need for peace.

But the headache was gone.

I looked up at the blue ceiling. Squinting, I watched little figures that appeared to be moving around. Were those things swimming on the ceiling? I blinked again. Fish, they were fish. How was that possible?

Then it hit me. The Galaftns. I was in their city.

I watched as a little orange fish scurried to catch up with the others that were ahead of him. I smiled, understanding how he felt.

The room was... aquatic. It didn't seem to be a medical bay, more like someone's bedroom. The sheets were white and soft. I wished I could just lie here forever. But I couldn't, I knew that. It was pathetic to even think it, especially knowing what I knew. There was an entire empire to get back under my rule and restore the peace that had been destroyed.

I swung my legs over the edge of the bed and examined the room more. The room was nicely decorated, but open. The only thing I saw was a desk and...

Emmerich.

He was asleep, his head slumped forward and his chest moving up and down. I wondered how long he had been waiting for me to wake up. How long was I out? I couldn't tell, especially since before all of this happened I didn't even know what day it was.

After everything, he was still by my side. I smiled as I watched him sleep, knowing he had probably spent hours worrying about me. He was sweet to me, more so than I deserved. Risking his life again and again to help me, he had left his home behind. I wanted to repay him, somehow, someday. I loved him with all my heart, and now I knew, he felt the same about me. I wished we were living another life, one without all this war, without responsibilities, and could just enjoy each other's company for the rest of our lives. But no matter what may come, all we needed was each other, and that strengthened me.

He had searched for me for an entire year before he saw me that day at Portland State University. I had felt an instant connection then, and now I knew I was right. All of that searching was because Michael had tried to kill me

That's right, the poison.

I tried to remember what had happened that caused me

to use the portal to go to Earth, but it still was all fuzzy. I remembered a large man laughing, chasing me as I tried to escape. His voice was deep but that was all I could remember before waking up in the hospital in Portland. It must be the poison keeping me from remembering.

I closed my eyes and processed what had happened before the poison had taken over. It still hurt that Michael had betrayed me. He tried to kill me twice, first with the poison and then he tried to shoot me in cold blood. I had known him all my life, he was like a brother, a best friend. Then just because of my decision for peace, he wanted to take over the empire.

How could he have betrayed me like that?

It made me sick to my stomach, that someone so close to me could just decide that I was no longer worthy of existence and would want to end my life. I could never do that to him, I could never kill him, even after all of this.

I didn't know who to trust, especially since I couldn't remember who had administered the poison on Michael's orders. At least I knew it wasn't Emmerich—he had gone to such lengths to keep me alive. If he wanted to betray me, he would have already. No, it was someone else that I had trusted.

Emmerich stirred. When he saw me watching him, he practically jumped out of his chair. "Angel, you're awake."

I nodded, glad that he was awake so we could talk. "It would appear so. Would you mind telling me where I am?" I knew we were underwater, but I wondered where in the Galaftns' city I was.

He sat down next to me on the bed. "Galaftns. We brought you straight here after you passed out. We didn't know what else to do. Since they manufactured the poison, we thought it was our best bet."

He was right, Michael had said that the poison was of Galaftn origin. They would most likely be the ones to have an antidote. "If I recall, aren't the Galaftns at war?"

"They are, but they also know Michael set them up to make it look like they had assassinated you. They knew if they helped you they could get their lives back. King Kwai still trusts you and knows that you wouldn't betray him. He made sure you were safe and had all of his best doctors making sure you were healed from the poison, along with Elwood's help, of course. They figured it must have stayed dormant in your system due to head trauma that also knocked out part of your memories. Once the memories came back, so did the effects of the poison."

I imagined Elwood running around frantically and helplessly as the other doctors took care of the poison. "I bet he was a bit too eccentric for their taste."

"He surprised them, yes, but tell me, how do you feel?"

"I feel... better. The headache is gone and my memory seems to have mostly returned, other than how I got to Earth. I remember the people clamoring for war, the promises Michael gave them behind my back."

He took my hand "What else do you remember?"

"Michael explained most of it when he captured me. How I was ruler of this planet, how he tried to kill me," I paused and looked up at Emmerich. "Us."

Emmerich stroked my hand. "I wanted to tell you so badly, but with the headaches, I didn't know what was going on."

"And you were right, I almost died didn't I?"

He nodded. "Thankfully they had the antidote at the ready."

"And what did you have to promise the Galaftns to get it? That I would help them defeat Michael? That somehow I could win over my people and get them to believe in me once again? There's no way, Emmerich, they don't have faith in me anymore."

"Don't say that. You are the ruler of Cartref, not him. Losing a year won't change that."

I wanted to believe him, but the truth was that I had lost control. Michael had tainted their minds. How else could my guards treat me like a prisoner? If they believed in Michael and what he stood for, why would they ever want to go back? "Do you believe that?"

He nodded. "Yes, I do. There are plenty of your people here in the Galaftn's city, waiting for your orders. They believe in peace and don't want Michael to rule any longer. You saw the Capital, it isn't thriving like it used to and people are beginning to understand why you didn't want to go to war."

"There are Cartrefians here, in this city? The Galaftns let them in even after all that's happened?" I questioned, not able to believe they would trust any of my people after what we had done.

"Yes, they believe that you can bring peace once more."

I let out a long breath, trying to rationalize why they would do such a thing. I tried to be a strong leader, yes, but that gave the Galaftns no reason to trust that I would follow through. How could they be so willing to lie down their defenses and welcome my people in after Michael declaring war on them?

"How long was I out?"

"Four days."

My eyes widened. "Four days? What happened?"

"Michael announced that you were still alive. He claims the Galaftns brainwashed you into helping them and declared you a traitor. He wants you taken alive, but by the looks of it, many want you dead."

I shook my head. "How could they think that? How could they be so ignorant to believe everything he says?"

Emmerich shrugged. "Michael is a very persuasive man, he can get people to believe whatever he wants them to. All it takes is charisma and a strong belief to get people to trust. It's a matter of power."

Did he have this planned all along, to get rid of me so he could rule? He had never seemed to care about power and leadership, he was always obedient and helpful. It wasn't until the Galaftns appeared that he changed for the worse. "Then he has already won."

"There are many that still fight for you," Emmerich explained. "And they're ready whenever you are."

"What if I'm not ready?"

"What do you mean? You understand the situation, don't you? The Galaftns trust you to help them restore peace; that you will do what you can."

"Yes, but..." I trailed off, trying to gather my thoughts. "I was never a strong enough leader to begin with, that's why Michael got rid of me. I'm not meant to rule."

Emmerich put his hand on my shoulder. "No, listen to me. You are a far better ruler than any of your ancestors. You are compassionate and care about your people.

Michael doesn't care, he just wants power. Many still follow you. I still follow you."

I looked up at him. Sincerity filled his eyes. He had always believed in me, I knew. It was just a shock, one moment being a girl with no memories, starting school for what felt like the first time, to having to rule an entire race and fight a war. It was overwhelming to think about and I just needed to have time to sort it all out.

"How can you still have faith in me when I couldn't even remember who you were?" I asked.

"Because I knew you would remember—I knew my Angel would come back for me," he kissed my forehead. I closed my eyes, taking in the warmth of his lips on my skin. It had been so long since he had kissed me. "You just need time to remember, this is probably just a lot to think about. I can understand that."

"It is. I don't know what to think. I don't know who to trust," I explained.

He brought his eyes to my level. "You can trust me. Know that I will always be here for you, through thick and thin. Whatever you want me to do, I will do it."

I smiled, feeling a little more secure after hearing that come out of his lips. I no longer felt lost and alone. I only had to remember who and what I could believe in.

"Elwood should come soon with some food. I want you

to eat and regain your strength. Stop worrying about everything else and just take a few breaths. With all that's going on, I understand that you want to panic. Just take one step at a time, all right?"

I nodded. "I'm glad you are here, Emmerich. I don't know what I would have done without you."

"Just stop the war once and for all, okay? That's all I ask."

If only it were that simple, if only I could overcome my fear that my people will look at me and see me as a weak leader for wanting peace, not war. It would take time and a lot of effort and might not even be possible after everything Michael had done. But Emmerich was right, I had to try. I had to stand up for what was right.

The door slid open and Elwood came in with a tray of food. The aroma filled the room, making my stomach grumble. Yes, food would bring some energy that I needed back, and by the smell of it, it would be tasty.

Emmerich kissed my forehead again. "I will be back later, all right? Then we can talk more. Enjoy your food for the time being."

I watched as he left, wishing that he would stay. I loved Elwood's company, but with Emmerich, I felt different, I felt...

Love.

"I hope you're hungry," Elwood put the tray on a small table and motioned for me to come sit at the nearby table.

I smiled. He was the only one in my family that had my back. The aircraft crash that had taken my parents, had also killed his. In the beginning we only had each other, and Michael, of course. At least Elwood was still at my side. Although I doubted he would ever betray me, I felt the fear linger in the back of my head. Was he the one that had poisoned me?

He placed the bowl down on my table and handed me a spoon. "Talpan soup. Your favorite."

This is what I was craving every time I ordered soup on Earth. I had tried so many types yet none of them ever hit the spot. Now I knew why.

I took a sip. The delicious sweet cream filled my mouth, along with scalding heat now pouring down my throat. I waved my hand back and forth, trying to cool off my tongue. "Hot, so hot."

Elwood handed me a glass of water. "Sorry, I should have warned you. I didn't know if you were awake and I didn't want to let it get cold so I heated it more than I should have."

I chuckled at his worry and my doubts about him disappeared. I couldn't believe that he would ever betray me. "Elwood, can I ask you something?"

He sat down in the chair next to me. "Anything."

"Why didn't you become Emperor when I disappeared? According to the laws of our society, a blood relative is to take power. Shouldn't the people have turned to you?"

Elwood ran his fingers through his short curly red hair. "I guess it has to do with Michael being smart, and a total ass. He knew the laws as well as either of us and had to get rid of me somehow. The moment you disappeared, I suspected he was behind it, but he acted faster than I did. By the time I could call the guards on him, he had already declared me an enemy of the Empire. He said I was working with the Galaftns and planted evidence to prove I had a part in the assassination."

"That's horrible," I whispered.

"Yeah, well, Michael is horrible. Luckily Emmerich put it all together and knew you weren't dead. He had complete confidence in finding you and stopping Michael once and for all. After Michael put Isaac and me in prison for the crime, Emmerich broke us out and we've been trying to help him find you. I don't know where he found you, or how, but he did. I have complete faith that we will overpower Michael and win this war. Then we can have peace, just like you wanted."

I got out of my chair and wrapped my arms around

him. I was so lucky to have had him by my side this entire time, and I was glad that he still stood up for me. "Thank you."

"Anything for my cousin." He rubbed my back. "I will always be by your side."

"How can you and Emmerich have so much faith in me?"

"Because you are a lot stronger than you believe. Don't you remember the fights we used to have as children? I recall getting beat to a pulp."

I laughed, remembering. "That's different."

"It isn't that you aren't strong, Angela, it's that you care so much about your people that you can't stand them getting hurt. And that, my cousin, makes you stronger than any of our ancestors."

Before I could respond to his statement, the door opened again. A tall bald figure walked in. His hands were webbed, his eyes white, and his skin was slick and light grey. He wore a long white robe that whisked the ground. This made him seem almost heavenly, as it appeared as if he was floating as he moved around. I stared in awe. It had been so long since I had seen a Galaftn.

And this wasn't just any Galaftn, but their leader, Kwai. I remembered meeting him before the kidnapping.

We had talked quite a few times, even though my people only met him with angst. Elwood and I stood and bowed.

"King Kwai, it is an honor to be in your presence. I offer my deepest gratitude for helping me in my time of need. Thank you, sincerely."

He motioned for me to sit back down. "There is no need for such formalities, Empress Starr, it is my pleasure to find you are well," his voice, like all Galaftns' voices, was melodic, almost like speaking in song. "Elwood, sir, would you mind if I talk to the Empress alone?"

Elwood bowed again. "Of course." With that, he left us. I sort of wished he could stay but I knew a discussion between leaders needed to be private. Even though I felt I could trust Elwood, we still had to be careful.

"I am pleased that you are back, for the past year this world has been in chaos," Kwai went on.

It ate at me, that so much had happened while I was on a different world, that I had been unaware. "Yes, so I have learned. I am sorry for my absence, but I had no memory of who I was."

"That is what Emmerich has told us. He has stayed in contact with our people since you disappeared, making sure that your belief in peace still gave us hope. We still have complete faith in you, and now that you are back and healthy, we may precede in regaining your power as

Empress."

"You still trust me, even after all of this?" I asked.

He nodded. "I have always had faith in you, Empress Starr, all my people have. We watched as your ancestors destroyed civilizations. But in you we saw something different. That was why we stepped foot on land, knowing you would bring peace to this world."

I couldn't believe what I was hearing. I never knew they had seen what my ancestors had done and that they would believe in me so much as to risk coming on land. "I think you made a mistake."

Kwai raised an eyebrow, at least where there should have been eyebrows. "Oh?"

I moved a strand of red hair away from my face. I had to be honest with him, I couldn't lie to a leader whom I considered to be a friend. "Honestly, I don't think I can sway my people. Michael has them so wrapped up in this war that I don't think they will trust that you want peace. That both of us want peace."

Kwai took a seat at the desk and steepled his webbed fingers together. "Do you really think that? Do you not trust your people?"

I turned and looked out at the ocean. I could see far into the dark abyss, the sapphire blue more beautiful than any gem ever could be. It seemed calm and pleasant but I knew what was happening above it. "Michael... He betrayed me. He turned my people against me. They wanted a fight, they wanted to go to war before he claimed you kidnapped me. How will I get them to take me back?"

"Empress Starr, have you ever wondered why your people turned to Michael?"

And why they betrayed me? How they could turn to someone else other than me? I had thought about it constantly since I had woken up. "Because they want war."

Kwai shook his head. "No, they don't. They want a powerful leader to tell them what they need. They look to someone for guidance. Although you were a good leader, you were never strong in the eyes of your people. That's where Michael has the advantage."

"You are right, I was weak. That's why I don't understand why you are putting so much hope in me."

"It's a matter of perspective, Empress Starr. I can see what others can't, and what I see is a true leader within you, you just have to find it," he explained.

I wished I could believe him, that inside myself stood a powerful, strong leader, but I didn't view it that way. No, I didn't believe that for an instant. "I grew up being told I wasn't strong enough to be a leader, that I wasn't good enough. My mother and father prayed for another heir until the day they died. When I finally made a decision that was my own, someone tried to kill me. How am I supposed to stand up for myself when all of that has happened? How am I supposed to believe in myself?"

"You are honest, and I like that about you. It's a quality I quite admire, you know why?"

I shook my head.

"Because you are one of the few that still have that virtue. Most people spin lies and give promises they cannot keep. You, on the other hand, are upfront about everything. Besides, there are plenty of people who follow you, who believe in you. You need to stop looking at those who betrayed you and look at those who have always stood by your side."

He was right. It was just so hard to see those who wanted to help compared to those who didn't believe in you, those who wanted to always bring you down. Their voices always seemed louder. "You mean like Emmerich? And Elwood?"

"They are a start, yes."

"I know that they believe in me, but that is the problem. I don't want to let them down. I want to be the person they see me as, but that is so hard.

"How do you know you will let them down unless you

try?"

Truth be told, I didn't. I glanced out the glass at the fish swimming around, watching as a beautiful purple and yellow one went by the wall. I was being weak, but it was a lot to take in after the last year. I couldn't let myself fail again and lose my throne. I felt like if I had been stronger, then none of this would have happened.

I didn't respond to his question, knowing he was right. I had to try for my people, I couldn't just stand by and let Michael throw the world into chaos. It was my turn to stand up and fight, just as Emmerich and Elwood had been doing for the past year.

Kwai tapped one of his long fingers on the desk as these thoughts were running through my mind. After a moment he gathered himself and stood up. "Come with me, I have something to show you."

I followed him out of the room, curious where he was leading me. King Kwai was an extraordinary being, I had always thought. He rarely spoke what was on his mind, but always seemed calm and decisive. I had hoped we could have bypassed this war and signed a treaty, but that wasn't the case. I was glad that after all this time, he still wanted peace with me and my people, even though my people had shown him nothing but prejudice and hatred.

As we walked down the hallways, I took in the beauty

that was the Galaftns' palace. The colors were subtle, blues and greens and some greys, while the walls that led to the outside were transparent so you could enjoy the sight of the ocean. I watched as fish danced around, and groups of Galaftn people moved around the city. Their city wasn't too large, nothing compared to Capital City, but that was understandable. My ancestors had many generations to expand our empire and had destroyed many other civilizations to get to where it was today.

While they didn't have a large city, the Galaftns had a great military. King Kwai had shown me their arms and technology, so he knew that I understood that if we went to war, even with their small numbers, they would put up a good fight. He knew he didn't need to show that to me, but as a leader, he had to make sure I acknowledged at what lengths he would go to keep his people safe. I admired that about him, and I felt the same way about my people.

Fish of all different shapes and sizes swam by the transparent walls. In the distance I saw some Galaftns swimming around near what appeared to be some kind of sport court. The Galaftns were special in that way, having both lungs and gills so they could breathe on land or in the water. It was why my kind had never seen them before. They had been hiding in fear that what happened to the Goedwig would happen to them.

My father and grandfather would have punished me if they knew I was allying with a leader from a different civilization. I was glad that I no longer had to live by their rules, and could try to make peace with other leaders, even though my people didn't want me to. They felt allowing new species of humans into the city would jeopardize our way of life. I had tried to get them to understand the importance of learning from other cultures and how the trade of goods and information would be beneficial to everyone, but then Michael had interfered. Now we were here, near the end of a very long battle.

King Kwai held open a door, and I walked into a large ballroom, jam-packed with both Galaftns and Cartrefians. I saw my men standing side by side with King Kwai's people, and for once I felt that I had some backing by my people. It brought tears to my eyes.

This was what King Kwai wanted me to see, that I shouldn't give up hope, that some understood what I was fighting for and were behind me all the way. Those gathered there didn't notice as King Kwai and I snuck into the back of the room, as all of them were facing the front, waiting for someone to stand up and talk to them. With King Kwai standing next to me, I wondered who they could have been waiting for.

The ballroom was loud as people spoke to each other about the end of the war coming soon. If they defeated Michael once and for all, they believed, they could finally bring peace to the empire. They even spoke of me and how the gods must have been on their side for me to come back and be healed. I couldn't believe that they still looked to me as a leader, after disappearing for so long, and for that I was grateful.

After a few moments, someone appeared on the stage near the podium. I squinted to get a better look and could just make out who it was. It was Emmerich. Everyone had been waiting for him, I couldn't believe it.

The crowd hushed as he readied himself for a speech he was about to make. I watched in amazement, never having seen him talk in front of a group like this. How much had he changed since I had disappeared? He cleared his throat and spoke.

"Michael has lied to all of us, he claimed the Galaftns kidnapped the Empress, but it was Michael himself who tried to kill her," Emmerich began, his voice firm and not wavering. A murmur rippled through the crowd. I heard people ask each other how such a thing could happen and how someone like him could ever have taken rule over the empire. "I know this because I found her just a few days ago, poisoned, and not remembering anything. A group of us got her here in time to be saved."

"Then where is she?" One man shouted from the middle of the ballroom. "She is our leader, why does she not speak to us herself?"

I knew I should have spoken up but I wanted to hear what Emmerich's response would be, how he would handle a situation like this. This was his turn to talk. I glanced over at King Kwai. He was as intrigued as I was in how Emmerich would act.

Emmerich didn't seem phased by the question but kept his calm. "She is resting. Michael had given her a powerful poison, and it made her body weak. We are lucky she is still alive. I have personally seen to it that she will be in perfect condition for this battle, don't worry. She will be with us soon."

"How do we know you aren't lying? How do we know this isn't some trick?" another person asked.

"Yeah, I want proof that she is alive, that she is still the leader that she once was. I don't want to put my trust in anyone other than her, not after what Michael did!" another person called out.

"Why would I lie to you?" Emmerich asked, and the room went silent once again. "You have turned against Michael's rule and looked to me for guidance. I did not make you come here, you knew that I stood for peace and equality from the start," he straightened his jacket before going on. "But one thing is for sure, we must bring down Michael's reign. We must stop him. This is our only chance, if we wait any longer he will have persuaded all the masses to attack the Galaftns head on. As people of both races, we cannot allow this!"

Everyone cheered. I watched as Emmerich worked up the crowd's morale. It impressed me that he stepped up after I disappeared and became the resistance's leader. He had changed so much from the boy I had found in the palace, confused and smarter than he would ever admit. He always said I had taught him so much about the universe, but I disagreed. Emmerich had taught me so much more. He had always been there for me, it was time that I returned the favor.

I knew what I needed to do, why King Kwai brought me to this rally. My people needed to see me stand up for them, to see I was there and that I would be their Empress once again. They had waited long enough.

Stepping forward, I made my way to the platform. Murmurs echoed across the ballroom as they noticed my approach and cleared a path, bowing. I kept my head up and smiled to them, letting them know that everything would be all right, that I was finally here to take lead.

I knew it wasn't Emmerich's job to guide these people,

it was mine and mine alone. I had to stand up and face the fact that this was where I belonged. I was thankful to have someone like King Kwai on my side, letting me see this for myself, understanding what a leader needed to see to regain their strength.

Emmerich gave me a grin as I stepped up on the stage. I placed my hand on his shoulder. "I've got it from here, Emmerich, thank you."

"My pleasure, Angel," he whispered for only me to hear. I peered out at the crowd. "Michael has broken one of the most sacred laws of our empire! He has betrayed me and used his power for evil and corrupted the people's beliefs. He is a traitor and must be stopped!"

The crowd roared, louder than I ever remembered hearing. I looked down at all who followed me, all who believed in me. I remembered what it felt like to be the Empress, to have people look up to me. They needed a leader, they needed me. And, luckily, I had friends to back me up if I were to falter.

"He has betrayed this empire!" I yelled out, the tension that had been building up inside me spilled out, strengthening me. "He has betrayed us all! And we will put an end to it!"

The crowd erupted into more cheers. I could see they all wanted to join up and help our empire be the powerful empire it once was. Galaftns and Cartrefians were standing together in this time of need and it brought so much joy to my heart.

"I am not my father, nor his father before him. I will not put up with unjust war, I will not put up with this discrimination." I nodded to Kwai, who I believed still to be in the back of the crowd. "With King Kwai's help, we will return peace to this planet, let no one live in fear, and move forward into a better empire!"

"We trust you with our lives, Empress Starr," a voice called out. "But do you have what it takes to defeat Michael and bring back order?"

It was a good question and just moments ago, I might not have been able to answer, but now I had an answer. "I have the support of my people and all those around me. I have faith, and with all of you and the Galaftns behind me, I believe we can take down Michael once and for all. I know that we must attack now before it is too late!"

"We have a plan," Emmerich interrupted. I glanced at him, surprised, remembering that he had mentioned this before. I still needed to be briefed on it, but was thankful that during the time I was out, they had already moved forward with military strategies. I presumed that King Kwai's men helped put together the plan. Knowing Emmerich, I knew it had to be foolproof. He was a smart lad, and I was very thankful he was on our side.

Emmerich went on. "We will attack the palace at midnight. We have assigned each of you to a unit and each of the unit leaders have their orders. We will have our empire back tonight, if it's the last thing we do!"

Loud cheers erupted and people began to separate into what I presumed to be their units. I could feel the excitement in the room as everyone hurried off, to get ready for battle. They were ready to fight to have peace once again. They were ready to put Michael in his place and go back to the world that they once knew.

As everyone left the ballroom, Emmerich took me aside and away from the microphone. He embraced me. "So you made it to our little meeting."

"I did. Thank you for saying what I needed to hear," I shoved Emmerich playfully. "Sure you were just a physicist on Earth? You seem to be more of a general."

Emmerich laughed. "My father was a general in Deutschland. It was one reason I left home, I didn't want to be drawn into that kind of life. My Mutter tried to get me to stay, but she knew I could never be happy there."

He hated war. I couldn't believe what I was hearing, he had never told me that was why he moved to the United States. I had always thought he had gone to the U.S. to study. Instead, I had put him where he didn't want to be.

"I'm so sorry, I didn't know. You could have said—"

He placed his hands on my shoulders and stopped me from going on. "This is different, though. This is worth fighting for. This is where I want to be."

He leaned in and kissed me on the lips.

"I see that you two are closer than ever," Elwood commented as he stepped on the stage.

I blushed, hating it when someone saw me show affection to Emmerich. I thought everyone had left.

Elwood gave me a hug. "I am glad that you are doing better, and that you were here for this. We didn't know if you would be well enough to attend."

King Kwai joined us in our conversation. "I knew seeing her people and how they support her would bring her energy back. Call it a leader's intuition."

I smiled. "Thank you, friend, I hope that this battle will bring us everlasting peace between our people, if not the entire world."

"As do I, Empress Starr. Now, I believe these two boys want to catch you up on the plan they have come up with. I will be with my people, readying them. I will see you before you leave?"

I nodded. "Yes, you will."

He returned the nod, and I watched as he left the ballroom.

"Now," I turned to Emmerich and Elwood. "Let me see this genius plan you developed."

Emmerich and Elwood led me to the briefing room that the Galaftns had set up in the palace for them. The rest of the men and the Galaftns were getting ready for the battle while they laid out the plan for me and went over the last details. It felt as if everything was moving so fast, but it was a good change from not knowing what was going on. I knew we needed to act fast to defeat Michael, so I tried to take in everything I could in the time that was given to me.

"Here is the plan we put together," Emmerich pointed at the map he had laid out on the table, as Isaac joined us, "While the main forces are attacking the palace, drawing most of the guards into battle to make sure no one gets near the palace, we will insert you, Isaac, and Elwood into the palace to get to Michael."

"What then?" I asked.

"We either get him to call off this war, or kill him," Elwood answered.

I bit my lip. Even after everything, Michael was still someone I held dear to my heart. We had grown up together, had always been at each other's side. Although he tried to kill me, I don't think I could do the same. "I don't think I can kill him. He was like a brother to me."

Emmerich shook his head, not able to believe what I was saying. "He tried to kill you, Angel. If you don't kill him, he will kill you. I can't let that happen."

"Just kill the little weasel and get it over with," Isaac added.

I gave him a look, but couldn't help but chuckle at him calling Michael a weasel. He was one, I had to admit, but hearing Isaac use that word was rather humorous. I shook my head. "No one deserves to die, not if I can help it."

"I'll try to keep that in mind," Isaac whispered under his breath.

I glanced at Isaac, curious about what he had meant by that. I felt a memory try to come to my mind, but there was no time to figure out what that itchy feeling was, we had a battle to wage. "What about the rest of my people?"

Emmerich pointed at the map. "I will command the armies below, making sure the distraction works."

He would leave me? I couldn't believe it, I didn't want that to happen. "You will lead them?"

He nodded, not meeting my eyes. "Yes. I have been leading them for a while, they look up to me. The only other person who they look up to is you, but you need to be stopping Michael."

I didn't want to be separated from Emmerich, not after

having almost lost him when I was in Portland. It was still a long time that I had been away from him and now that I could remember who he was, I didn't want to spend another minute apart. "Why can't Isaac do that and you come with Elwood and me?"

"Because they trust me and know that I can lead them to victory. We have been planning for a very long time, I know it better than anyone else. If we want this to work, I have to be out there making sure you can get in with no trouble," he stroked my cheek with his hand. "Don't worry, Angel, I will be careful. The sooner you three defeat Michael, the sooner all of this will be over."

I nodded. He was right, he needed to lead the people into battle and it was up to me to bring Michael down. Even though I had been trained for war my entire life, never did I think I would have to fight for my throne and for peace.

"Don't worry," Isaac slapped his hand on my back. "I'll keep ya' safe."

When Isaac said that, I felt less than reassured that everything would be all right. Isaac had been close to Michael, and it surprised me he had found himself on this side of the battle. He was a strong warrior, so I was happy he was on our side, but I had this aching feeling that it would be better if Emmerich was with me instead of

Isaac.

"And I will be with you," Elwood added and slapped Isaac's back as well. "But I don't think I can take them down like tree-stump here."

Isaac turned to him and glared. "What is that supposed to mean?"

Elwood shrugged. "Nothing. Just that you are big, and strong. Like a large tree."

I laughed at their bickering. I remembered it well from before, the two of them never seemed to get along. Elwood always loved joking with Isaac, it was fun to watch since Isaac would always get so mad and could hurt Elwood. Hell, he could probably beat Elwood with just his pinky finger. Even with all this chaos, some things never changed.

Once the briefing was over, I headed to the hangar to check on the progress of my men. The Galaftns had stolen a bunch of ships from our junkyards and repaired them. They knew how to recycle parts very well and once this battle was over, I would need their expertise to help strengthen both our armies. It would be great to have their knowledge on our side and be able to reuse material like they do.

The war ships were from my grandfather's time—large, heavy, and very slow. Now after the Galaftns' reconditioning, they still had the strong armor, but were stealthy and fast. I could see the amazement on each of my men's faces as they helped put the finishing touches on the ships. They were impressed.

We readied for battle, knowing we would only have one chance. The tension was palpable throughout the entire city. Thousands of King Kwai's men had vowed their allegiance to me and I felt honored they still believed in me, despite the actions of my people. I was lucky to have such a great nation on my side.

I did everything I could to help, to make sure my men were ready for battle. They insisted they were, but I could feel their fear in the air, along with the excitement that everything was coming to a head. I was afraid for them and the rest of the people in Capital City. I hoped they would see the truth that Michael wasn't the leader they saw him as, and that peace was always better than war.

I found King Kwai with his men, helping them with anything they needed, as if he were one of them instead of their leader. He was very compassionate, knowing he couldn't act like he stood above them all but was at the same level as them.

He nodded to me. "Empress Starr, I take it you are feeling better now?"

"Yes, thank you for all your help. I hope that this battle

succeeds so we may be great allies. We have much that we can teach each other, I have a feeling that our two species can live in harmony, given the chance."

"Your people are lucky to have such a leader as yourself. I am sure that Emmerich will do a fine job leading them into battle. He is a very strong man, you are lucky to have him on your side," he explained.

"Yes, I know. He is a blessing to us all. I am glad he stood up when I couldn't," I agreed, the thought of him bringing a warm sensation in my chest.

King Kwai stepped closer. "You two are in love, aren't you?"

I blinked, surprised. "I... uh..."

"I thought so. I just wanted to say you have nothing to worry about while he is leading the battle. He will be okay. Keep your mind on your own mission and the faster you finish, the faster this will all be over."

I nodded, knowing he was right. I had to do my part and not worry about Emmerich. I understood that he needed to be there leading the soldiers into battle. He was a born leader, even though he had never wanted to be one.

King Kwai went back to his men. I did the same and made sure that my own men needed nothing from me.

Although the talk with King Kwai had made me feel

better, I was still worried about Emmerich—that we wouldn't see each other again. After everything that we had been through, I was afraid that this could be the end. If that was true, then Michael would have won. He would have destroyed the one thing I cared about most. I cared about my people a lot, but Emmerich was the one who was always there for me, through thick and thin. If I were to lose him, I didn't know what I would do. I would be strong for him, I supposed, and know that he would want me to lead with my head held high no matter what.

I checked up on my men, seeing if they needed any help. They all seemed to be fine, not needing my help as they readied their own ships and suited up for the fight. Lasers were energized, engines were checked, and defense mechanisms were double-checked. It all seemed to be running smoothly with Emmerich and King Kwai's lead.

All of this made me feel a little helpless. If they could do all this, did they need me? Emmerich had said they did, that the people wanted me leading them. I had seen everyone at the rally. It made me feel warm inside that they cared that much about me, that they still looked up to me as being the true leader.

Suiting up in my white and orange jumpsuit, I made sure my dryll—what they would have called guns on

Earth—were charged and ready to go. I strapped two on
my legs and one behind my back. I couldn't be too
careful, it was all or nothing. I also had a knife in my
boot. Primitive compared to the dryll, but I knew it could
come in handy.

As I finished up, Emmerich came over to the ship I had
been helping to prepare with Elwood and Isaac. He
leaned against the doorframe. "Are you ready to do this?"

I looked at him and smiled. He appeared as handsome
as ever, a bit of grease smeared across his face and in his
blonde hair. I wiped it off his cheek with my thumb. "As
ready as I will ever be."

He stroked my hand. "I love you Angel, don't you ever
forget that."

I leaned in and kissed him. "I love you too,
Emmerich."

He wrapped his arms around me and held me. I wished
for a moment that the world would stop and we could
stay like this forever. His warm body chased away any
coldness that had crept inside of me. I felt strong when he
was near, as if I could do anything. I tried to hold on to
that feeling, knowing once he stepped off the ship, it
would slip away. No, I wouldn't allow that. I would stay
strong for him, for me and all of my people.

After a moment, Emmerich backed away and kissed

my forehead. "I have to go. We are leaving soon, Elwood and Isaac will join you."

I nodded, trying to hold back the tears. "Will you promise to be careful?"

"I will. Just follow the plan, all right? To the letter. Then everything will be just fine."

"Whatever you say."

He smiled as he placed his hand on my cheek. I rested my hand on his and enjoyed the warmth once more.

"After all this, we will go somewhere. Just you and me," he said

"That sounds like a plan. We will go somewhere we have never been before, I know of some great beaches on the other side of Cartref."

Emmerich kissed me once more, long and hard. I wrapped my arms around him, not wanting to let him go. He drew back, and I reached out for him, but knew I couldn't keep him there.

"I have to go now. Elwood and Isaac will take care of you, I promise."

I couldn't say anything, in fear that the tears would come. I nodded.

With that, he left me. I stood there, in the doorway, half hoping he would come back, but I knew he wouldn't. I turned back to finish getting ready.

It wasn't long before Isaac and Elwood arrived, also ready to fly out. It was T-Minus one hour before we would begin our attack.

Elwood saw the seriousness on my face as I tried to hold back all the emotions that were trying to escape me. "Are you all right?"

I turned to him and nodded. "Yes, now let's get this war over with."

Our ships were old fighters from the Goedwig war. It amazed me the Galaftns had given them these upgrades, including additional thrusters to increase their speed. Technology had evolved since the Goedwig war, after all. Despite their sleek design, they could take a beating. In fact they were stronger than those we flew now, which were lighter, but not as sturdy. These were like the tanks on Earth that Emmerich had told me about.

I admit at first I was a little afraid to board the old ships —I couldn't believe they were made to fly again. I thought the only thing they were good for was scrap metal and homes for scavengers.

I hoped I was wrong.

They had changed the ships to move in both air and water. How, I had no clue, I wasn't an engineer. Emmerich probably helped with the design, and I was sure that the Galaftns knew a thing or two on how to make underwater machines.

They must have been working on this plan for a while, not just since my appearance back onto this world. Emmerich must have turned to them right away, knowing they trusted me and they had nothing to do with the assassination. It surprised me they would take Emmerich's word that he wanted to help them, especially after everything Michael had done. They must have seen he was sincere, not to mention Emmerich could charm his way out of any situation. He had a smile most politicians would die for. They must have had everything in place for this battle, all they needed was to find me.

It was crazy to think just a week ago I had been on Earth, not remembering any of this. I was a college student, thinking I had no idea where my life was heading. Life seemed so much different now, as if that experience wasn't even real. It was an eye-opener, though, to see how different life could be. If I ever went back, people would think I was crazy. My counselor Mandy probably would assume I had a traumatic experience. I understood why Emmerich didn't want to return, because no one would believe where he had gone. I know I couldn't live like that.

Now I wouldn't let anything stop me from having a

future on this planet. Not even Michael.

Elwood, Isaac, and I were all ready to go in the remodeled Goedwig warship. Our pilot went through the checklist, as did all the other ships. I could hear the radio crackle as he gave the order to launch. I realized I was trembling slightly, as I had never flown into a battle before, although it wasn't like I had never been close to losing my life before. Father would always talk about how gruesome war was, and I just hoped I would have the stomach to follow through. I knew it was the only way to stop Michael. So I took a deep breath and prepared for what was ahead of me.

"You ready for this Angela?" Elwood asked as the pilot was just finishing the pre-flight check.

I grinned. "For once, I am."

He nodded to the pilot, and he spoke into the speaker. "This is Star Leader. We are ready to go."

An ear-piercing warning siren echoed through the bay. Finally, after a minute it stopped and water began to pour into the hangar, submerging the ships. It was just like a hangar in space, except instead of a vacuum, it let in water. I watched as the water rose, making the aircraft sway back and forth. Once we were completely underwater, the hangar doors opened up completely, and craft after craft moved out into the vast ocean and headed for battle.

Our own craft swayed back and forth as we began to move out. I let out a breath that I didn't know I had been holding and we began to ascend towards the surface of the ocean.

We rose out of the sea and into the air. Water poured off the wings of the craft and fell back into the ocean. I watched as my fighters became airborne, glad their design was sound and the craft could both fly in air and travel through water. It was one of my biggest worries. The engines switched to thrusters, and we were on our way.

The city was in the near distance, I could see the palace in skyline, as beautiful as it always was. I wished it wouldn't have ended like this—with me having to take down my best friend. The city was stunning in the sunlight, and it was a city I wanted to protect. I had to do this even if it meant fighting my friend.

It wasn't long before some of Michael's fighters that had been waiting for us showed up. Their craft started firing lasers at us and our people fired back. I watched as a ship from each side exploded, metal chunks raining down on the water below. My heart ached for the lives of both crews. Even though they fought for Michael, they were still my people. Either way I would lose a lot of men whom I considered to be mine today.

More and more of Michael's craft appeared and lasers rained down on each side of the battle. Ships moved back and forth, zigzagging to avoid getting hit. Although our ships could take a beating and could outmaneuver theirs, it seemed Michael's men were expecting our next move. More of our ships crashed into the water below.

Elwood must have noticed my nervousness. "It will be okay, this is what they swore to do. They knew the risks. We are fighting for a better world."

I understood but it didn't make the pain go away. I still couldn't believe how many people were willing to die for me. I was both proud and scared—worried that this could be all for nothing and that we would lose. But I wouldn't give up, I knew. I would have faith that this plan would work. "I know, but it doesn't mean I don't feel for them. It's what separates me from Michael. I care about everyone's lives."

We stayed back, four large warcraft surrounded us, protecting us. Lasers fired at Michael's men if they came near. The Galaftns' crafts circled the warcrafts, making sure no one came close to my craft, their goal was protecting me so that we could stop Michael. I felt helpless as I watched, unable to do anything other than wait to get to the palace. I took a deep breath as I watched a Galaftn craft get hit, black smoke pouring out of the cockpit. It crashed into one of Michael's ships, as if with their last breath, they took out an enemy. I believed on Earth they called it a Kamikaze maneuver.

This line of Michael's defense began to dwindle in numbers. Although it felt as if we had lost our whole squadron, I looked out the glass to find many more ships rising out of the water and entering the battle. I was surprised at the numbers, but they had been assembling the army since I had disappeared, with many Cartrefians joining Emmerich's cause. Now we would see if all the effort was worthwhile, but I trusted that it was. I trusted that this plan would work.

Michael's men started to retreat into the city where I knew another line of defense would be waiting. We followed, many craft ahead of us, chasing off any of Michael's men. The four warcraft lead the way and we trailed behind. This was only the beginning, I knew. Once we entered the city, many more ships would appear and the battle would begin in earnest.

As we flew toward the city, I waited for the automatic guns of the city defense system to be triggered. It didn't happen. Emmerich had mentioned a man on the inside who would stall the defenses. Also, since some craft were

Cartrefian, it would take a while for the guns to register them as a threat.

I wondered how long they could delay the guns. I prayed it would be a while. If we were lucky, the battle would be over and I wouldn't have to worry about any more of me or my men or the Galaftns getting hurt. I just hoped Michael would listen to reason, and surrender before it was too late.

We entered the city. I watched as people ran in fear. Did they think we would attack innocent civilians? Had Michael brainwashed them into believing such a thing? Then again, if I saw hundreds of ships in the sky, I would take cover too.

The enemy flew at us in waves. The ship shook as a lucky shot made its way through the defenses and hit the hull of our ship. I grimaced, waiting for another blow to our ship. I was sure that we were done for. One of the Galaftn crafts surrounding us shot it down.

"That was close," I breathed.

Isaac gave me a sideways glance. "Yeah, well, it isn't over. We aren't even to the capital palace yet."

Elwood gave him a look. "Don't say things like that, we have to keep up hope. We will make it through fine, we have been preparing for this for a year now."

"Yeah, well, I am just trying to be realistic," Isaac said.

Elwood stuck his tongue out at Isaac and Isaac returned the gesture. I was glad the pilot wasn't looking back here, I didn't want to be seen with these two idiots. I smiled as I watched them bicker. I was glad that they were both by my side. I could always count on Elwood to lighten the mood and make me worry less, even if it was just for a moment.

I looked back out the glass. Some ships in the battle got hit and crashed down into the city. I tried not to watch, a sickening feeling filling my stomach. I hated to think that bystanders would get hurt in this battle, but I tried to remember that it wasn't my fault, that Michael had taken over and had disastrous plans for our world.

Capital City seemed a lot larger as we flew over the towering buildings that made up the city. It had been a long while since I had flown through the city, conscious that is, although both times I had been fearing for my life. The city appeared different from what I remembered, Michael's rule had not cared for it like I had. While I had made sure there was an equal opportunity for everyone and every area was thriving, now areas were desolate and abandoned, especially near the sea wall that separated the city from the ocean.

I looked back out at the warcraft that surrounded us. Emmerich was in one of them, making sure nothing happened to me. It reminded me of all the science fiction movies and series I had watched on Earth, yet here it was real. I could only imagine what people on Earth would think if they knew that somewhere in space, these things were actually happening.

The battle raged on, I still felt helpless as all I could do was wait for the chance to get through the line of enemy craft and hop into the palace and get to Michael. Every once in a while the ship would shake from a laser strike. Someone always came to the rescue, though, making sure that was all the damage they could do.

"Do you think stopping Michael will end this battle? How do we know the people will see the defeat and stop fighting?" I asked both Isaac and Elwood, hoping one of them would have the answer.

Elwood nodded. "I believe that once they see the truth, that you are more powerful than Michael and that you are their true leader, the battle will stop. Michael has been coveting that throne long enough, he won't go down without a fight but I believe you can stop him. We will be there by your side as well to back you up. Whatever you need, just let us know."

I looked at Isaac. He didn't say a word but I guess he agreed. His mind seemed to be somewhere else. I presumed he was thinking about the surrounding battle, wanting to be out there fighting himself just like the rest of us. But he needed to help me and Elwood, we couldn't do this alone.

"I want to tell you guys thank you for everything, I don't know what I would have done without you. I am glad you are on my side and I just hope that after all this is over, we will celebrate our victory over some drinks," I said.

Elwood nodded and smiled. "Something hard, might I add. And smooth."

"Definitely. And a nice meal to go with it," I glanced at Isaac but he still seemed to be caught up by what was happening outside the glass. "What sounds good to you Isaac? Or do you steer clear of the hard stuff?"

He turned to me, his eyes still dark. "Yeah, something hard for sure."

I didn't say another word as I looked back out at the fight that was going on around me. I couldn't believe all of this was happening still, and that Michael would go to such lengths to keep his power. He wouldn't succeed, I would make sure of that.

Michael's men seemed to dwindle in numbers and we were approaching the palace. The automatic guns still hadn't fired, and I was very thankful for that. I could make out the palace now, the beautiful architecture and sculptures making it appear as grand as ever. Never had I thought I would attack my home, needing to sneak in and reclaim it. So many of my ancestors had the world in their hands and I was the first to let someone take it away. Did that make me weak? I didn't think so. No, it strengthened me since I was one who had to fight for it.

A second wave of Michael's ships appeared and started to attack. It wasn't a surprise, I figured they would send out more once we reached a certain line. One of the lead crafts blocked a laser that was aimed for our craft and exploded right before my eyes. My stomach churned. I hated to see such a thing happen, but I had to be strong for my people. I wouldn't turn back now.

We began our descent to the palace, separating from the other craft with a squad in front of us clearing a path. I tried not to throw up when the pilot started defensive maneuvers, twisting and turning to evade fire. It had been a while since I flew in such a way. I remembered why I had hated it so much. I didn't like not being in control. Not to mention I couldn't keep my eye on the horizon when it kept moving all around.

A blast hit the ship and alarms started blaring. I gulped, hoping the pilot could deal with whatever damage it had caused. I believed that he could, I had faith that he could fix whatever the problem was. A couple of moments later, the beeping stopped. I took a deep breath.

Spinning around again, I gulped down the bile that filled my mouth. Damn motion sickness, I would have to work on mastering it after this was all over, just in case I had to fly like this again.

A couple of the ships in our squad got hit, and I watched as they dropped down to the city. For one of them, I saw a man parachute out of the ship. At least he was safe, but I wasn't sure about the other one. I hoped that Emmerich was safe. His was a much sturdier ship, and could take a lot more laser power than the ship I was in, that was why they had so many ships surrounding us, making sure we were all right. The larger ships were decoys, most of the people thinking I would be in one of them. I had seen the same thing on an episode of Star Wars. It seemed to work for them, why wouldn't it work for us?

The ship shook again, and I glanced out the glass, seeing as we were getting closer to the palace. It felt as if I could almost touch the end of this battle. All I had to do was make it and stop Michael. It was all I had to do and I would focus on that.

I watched as my people fought alongside us, taking down many of Michael's men. I was proud of them, standing up for what they believed in, standing by my side. I just hoped I wouldn't let them down. No, I wouldn't. I would take on Michael and I would not let anything stand in my way of defeating him.

"We are almost to the palace," Elwood said. "It will get a bit shaky as we fly in. Once we are within distance, you and Isaac will head out. I will be right behind you."

I nodded and started to suit up, with my hedfan strapped to my waist. It was a cool apparatus that helped decrease acceleration as you jump off of things. The hedfan differed from a parachute, and was a lot more expensive. It let the person jumping off guide themselves with better ease. I could only imagine what people would use them for on Earth. We were planning to jump out of the aircraft onto the roof of the palace. If Emmerich's intel was correct, it should be unguarded and unarmed. Once all of this was over, I would make sure the palace and defenses were a lot stronger, with Emmerich's help and the Galaftns, I think it will be the safest place in the entire system.

Isaac and Elwood also got ready with their hedfans. I was glad they were with me—I don't think I could have done this by myself. They made me feel stronger.

"Ready? Almost there!" the pilot yelled back to where we waited.

"Ready!" Isaac shouted back before I could say no.

The door opened, and I looked down. Did I mention I was afraid of heights? Maybe I just didn't notice until now, but I was afraid of heights. Or maybe it was just jumping. Yes, I had a fear of jumping. A fear of jumping out a moving vehicle hundreds of feet in the air towards the top of a palace.

Well, here's to facing my fears.

I closed my eyes and jumped. The hedfan let me land without breaking every bone in my body. I made a mental note to send a hundred roses to whoever invented it after this was over. The air rushed past me as I dropped to the roof below. Even with the hedfan, as I landed, I found that I would still have a few bruises, but at least I was alive. I got to my feet and waited for Isaac and Elwood to do the same.

Isaac came behind, it amazed me that the hedfan could hold back his heavy body as he plummeted down toward the palace. He landed gracefully on his feet, as if he had done it a hundred times. I just hoped he didn't see how pathetic I looked when I landed.

Not long after Isaac landed, Elwood also came down from the sky. He wasn't as graceful and was definitely related to me. He hit the roof with his foot, tumbled forward, and landed on his face. Luckily the impact wasn't that great and he would only be bruised for a few days.

Elwood stood up. "I'm fine, everything is okay! No one saw that."

Isaac hit him in the back of the head. "Idiot, how many times have I taught you how to jump out of a moving vehicle?"

"About ten, maybe twenty? I didn't break anything this time." He rubbed his head. "Head hurts though."

I threw my fist up in triumph. "We made it!"

Elwood high-fived me and as I turned to Isaac, I saw Isaac frown.

"What is it? What's wrong?" I asked.

He pulled out a dryll and pointed it at both Elwood and me. I stared at him, not being able to understand what he was doing. Why did he want to point the dryll at me? Why was he acting strange suddenly?

"Isaac, what are you doing?" I asked, raising my hands as if I was calming a ravage dog.

His eyes were dark. "Shut it, Angela. I don't take orders from you. Not anymore," he snarled.

The memory came back, flashing in front of my eyes. The man who poisoned me stood in front of me, with the needle used to inject me. It had to go straight into the bloodstream, I remembered. I struggled out of his grip and stumbled down the hallway, vision blurred, toward where Emmerich kept the device to open the portal. I wasn't thinking straight but I knew I had to go somewhere no one could find me.

So I had gone to Earth.

And I remembered the man who tried to hold me down and inject the poison into my arm.

That man was Isaac.

"You! You were the one who tried to kill me!" I couldn't believe it, I couldn't believe he had sided with Michael. I had known they were close, but Isaac worked for me, or so I'd thought. He was one of my men, yet his loyalty had been with Michael all along.

He laughed. "And thankfully you didn't remember what I did until now! Then all of this would have been for nothing. Then again, if you had tried anything, I probably would have just killed you. Couldn't let anyone know who I really worked for."

"Why?!" I exclaimed. Committing treason wasn't something someone woke up wanting to do. I wondered what Michael had promised him.

"Money, power, anything I wanted really. Michael is a very persuasive man, if you didn't already know. He knew that I wanted to be more than just one of your commanders, so he gave me, what you would call, a raise, all I had to do was kill you with the poison he gave me. Unfortunately you got away, but the poison was already in your system. I chased you, but you disappeared in Emmerich's room somehow. That's when I found the remote to open the portal thing, and Michael figured out how to re-open it. I found you again on Earth, unfortunately there were bystanders there so I couldn't finish the job."

That was the people on Earth who had found me on the road and took me to the hospital. Luckily the poison somehow became dormant so that Emmerich could find me. I must have hit my head on something that made the memories also suppress along with the poison. "That's how Michael found out about Earth, it was when I disappeared."

"Earth?" Elwood asked. "What is Earth?"

"It is where little Angela ran off to, an entirely different planet. But yeah, he made me spy on Emmerich since he knew he would go looking for you since I didn't finish the job. Took a while to find you though, and get the remote to work again. I don't know how Emmerich got to you first, if he had another remote or just followed my men to Earth. Either way, he has been a great pain in my ass. But it doesn't matter, I can finally claim my reward from Michael," Isaac gestured to the door. "Now, let's go."

"How could you do this? What is wrong with you? " Elwood shouted.

"Oh, yeah?" Isaac glanced at Elwood. "What are you going to do about it, pip-squeak? Not like you have ever been strong in a fight, or as a leader. Why didn't you lead the forces instead of Emmerich? After all, you were the rightful heir after Angela disappeared. You could have led the troops without her. You are just a weakling, always have been, always will be."

Elwood shook his head. "No, you are wrong. You are the one who is weak, giving in to money and wealth. At least I will always stand up for what is right." He reached for his dryll.

Isaac was right, though, he was stronger. With his quick reflexes, Isaac shot him twice in the chest, then turned the dryll back to me before I could even realize what had happened. I watched Elwood drop to the ground, his body slumping forward, blood pooling on the ground beneath him.

"No!" I started toward him, even though I knew it was too late.

"Don't move, Angela. I'm not supposed to kill you, but don't think I won't hurt you. He's dead, there isn't anything you can do. He had it coming for a while now," Isaac said as if he didn't even care. All the bickering—I had always thought they were friends. Then again, I had made that mistake before.

I stared down at Elwood's body. How could such a lively soul disappear so quickly? I would miss his cheerfulness and it felt as if part of me had died with him. I felt a tear trickle down my cheek. He was my cousin, my dear cousin who had always believed in me. He sacrificed himself for me. I couldn't let him down. I would stop Michael no matter the cost. I would avenge my cousin and I would take back my world. I lost too many lives today and I would not let them die in vain. The death felt like it activated the warrior inside of me, the one that had been dormant in my genes. I would not give up.

Isaac grabbed me and took my drylls I had armed myself with. He didn't know about the knife tucked in my boot, thankfully, and I wasn't going to mention it. I just hoped I would have the chance to use it either against him or against Michael.

"Now," he motioned toward the palace. "Let's go."

I spat at his feet. He slapped me across the face.

"Don't mess around, Angela! I told you I had no reason to hurt you. Don't give me an excuse."

I glared at him for a moment, then did as he said and entered the palace. Guards were waiting for us and joined

Isaac to escort me to the man himself.

Michael.

Neither Isaac nor I said a word on the way to Michael's office. My office. I knew that anything I could have said would make Isaac just hit me again. I needed my strength for when I would face Michael. I could take him down, even with none of the help I thought I had. Why? Because I had faith in myself, I had faith that for once I could be strong enough to step up to Michael and bring him down once and for all.

The hallways were quiet as we strode down them toward the office. Other than the guards who had joined us when we stepped inside, I had seen no other people. They were all probably stationed outside or up in the sky helping to battle against my people and the Galaftns in this war. Did they realize what they were fighting for was wrong? Or did they do what was told of them, in fear that Michael could order their death? I wondered if we had a man inside the palace or if Isaac had set this up all along.

When we went into the lifts, I no longer felt as if I was being thrown around. I remembered how this technology moved back and forth and understood how lights warned which way the lift would turn. It was only a matter of moments before we found ourselves on the correct floor where Michael was waiting.

The dark blue hallways seemed dimmer than ever, shadows moved across the ground, as if they knew what was to come. Although I didn't want to kill him, I knew at the end of this, only one of us would make it out alive. If the other lived, the battle would never end.

The guards took their sentry positions outside the door as we entered Michael's office. It was just the three of us now. Michael sat with his feet up on the desk, smiling as we walked in, oblivious to the chaos outside. I could see ships exploding behind him through the glass wall, but he didn't care about the lives being lost right outside his window. All he cared about was having his prize: me and my throne.

"Why, Angela, what a lovely surprise." He took his feet off the table and stood up. I had never seen him in such a happy mood, which made me even angrier, and disgusted. All that death that was just beyond that glass, yet he had a smile on his face. He reminded me of Loki, the ancient Viking god striving to be the ruler and only causing chaos —he definitely did not have the right to rule anyone.

I glanced around before answering, trying to calm myself down and keep a level head. There, above the fireplace still hung the picture of my grandfather. I recognized him now and remember the war that he had fought in. The war that brought Michael's people under Cartrefian rule. I wished that war had never happened, that none of my family was like the monster that he was. But they all were, except for me. "You aren't going to get away with this Michael, mark my words."

"Oh really? You mean the air raid that your dear Emmerich and Galaftns have started? The one Isaac warned me about? That reminds me," he pressed a button on the desk. "Markus, will you tell the guards it is time to push back the attack? Oh, and start up the automatic guns while you are at it. It's about time we show them who is truly powerful."

I stared at him, unable to believe my ears. So I was right, there was no person on the inside, it was all part of Isaac's treachery. The automatic weapons were functional and we would be destroyed in a matter of seconds.

"Yes sir," came the reply.

Michael grinned. "Thank you," he turned back to me. "Now the war has begun."

I watched as hundreds of craft came out of nowhere and began to attack my people and the Galaftns. I covered my mouth in horror as many of them were shot out of the sky. Even the warcraft were having trouble keeping aloft under the relentless fire. I knew some ships had made it into the palace, but Michael's men may have already gotten to them. We had lost the only weapon we truly had —the element of surprise. We were screwed.

Not able to keep my eyes from the glass, watching as many more craft crashed into the city. A fire had started in the distance. My city was being destroyed, and it was all because of Michael. How I wanted to punch him right then and there but with Isaac's dryll pointed at me, I knew I wouldn't get far.

One of the warcraft seemed to be wavering a bit in the sky. I prayed to the gods it wasn't Emmerich's. I couldn't tell from this distance. Our craft were trying to retreat back toward the ocean, but they were encircled by a legion of Michael's ships. We were done for.

"Why?" I whispered.

"I already told you, I don't believe in your ideas of peace. The Cartrefians demand power, to be the strongest beings on this planet! We can't allow the Galaftns to take over. We can't."

"They aren't trying to take over!" I yelled back. I was sick of his sadistic view of the world. I was sick of war and death. "We are saving each other the misery of a war! We are bypassing the grief and sorrow of losing our people! But you have brought all of that upon my city and I will not allow it!"

He shook his head and came out from behind his desk.

"You think you can trust them? Do you remember what the Goedwig did? Do you remember why your grandfather attacked them? Because they wanted to hurt us just like the Galaftns! You are more naïve than your parents gave you credit for."

I attacked him. I don't know what came over me, but I tackled him onto the ground before I even knew I had done it. I was tired of people calling me weak. I was fed up with it all. It was my turn to fight back—and as an alternate to words, I decided to use my fists. I guess it triggered memories of when we used to fight as children, because I punched him again and again in the face like an angry child. But instead fighting over a toy, I was hurting him because he had destroyed so much goodness and innocence in this world, and no longer deserved to give me that smile, to have my trust or my friendship. At that moment I realized I couldn't let him live a moment longer.

Isaac pulled me off of Michael before I did any real damage. He did have a bloody nose though, which I was rather proud of.

Michael tried to staunch the blood coming out of his nose. "You hit me," he said in disbelief, unable to comprehend the fact I had caught him off guard.

"You deserved it, and you know what?" I quickly

pulled the knife out of my boot and stabbed Isaac with it, slicing him in the throat. I didn't hesitate to kill him, not after what he did to Elwood—and to me. I was sick of being helpless, and of being nice and sweet. This was war, and I was finally facing it. He made a gargling noise as he fell dead at my feet.

I grabbed his dryll and pointed it at Michael. "You are a dead man."

Michael stared at me for a moment and then started clapping. "My my, has our Angela finally grown up?"

I waved the dryll again. "Don't mess with me, Michael! I mean it!"

He laughed as he came closer, ignoring my threat. "I don't think you have it in you to kill me."

I gestured to Isaac's body. "Want to bet?"

He stopped and looked at me appraisingly. "If I had known you would go to such lengths for your empire, I don't think I would have tried to kill you."

"What, did you think I would just stand by and watch you rule? Watch you destroy this planet and bring war and chaos wherever you went?"

He shrugged. "Truthfully? Yes. Even once I knew you were back, I didn't really think you would go to these lengths. I mean, I knew Emmerich had an army, but that didn't mean you would lead it or come after me yourself.

I'm impressed, Angela, you actually are standing up for what you believe in."

"I will always stand up for what I believe in. I always have. I never let you or my parents tell me what to think or say—or how to lead—and you know that."

"Yes, yes, and it has made you so weak. Look at us now, if you were anything like your ancestors, you would have never let me get this far."

I shook my head. "Don't make me tackle you again." I pointed at the speaker. "Call off the attack. Tell your men to stand down."

Michael did as I said and reached for the intercom. He pushed the button. "Markus, tell the men to stand down."

"Sir?"

"Do as I say."

"Yes, sir."

Michael gestured to the window, and I watched as his men left the battle. I had won. After all of this, I finally had beaten him. I took a deep breath. It was over.

Of course, it could never be that simple.

The door behind me opened and as I turned, Michael slammed something into my back. I hit the ground and my dryll slid across the floor. Michael grabbed it.

"Ah, ah, Angela. I don't think so," he pointed it at me. "You need to learn to keep your eyes on your opponent."

I glanced over to see Markus. So he did have a backup plan. I was impressed—mad that I hadn't thought of it. But it didn't mean the fight was over. No, this was just the beginning.

"Is that everything sir?" Markus asked.

"Yes, that will be all," Michael responded.

I glanced back at the window. His ships were back. I was a fool. Michael had always been one step ahead of me. I didn't know what to do—he had me exactly where he wanted me.

"So this is it? You're going to kill me?"

He shook his head. "No, I think making you watch as your people suffer will be even better." Michael slammed his foot down on my right hand. I screamed. "In case you have another hidden knife, I want to make sure you can't use it."

I cradled my broken hand and looked up at him. "You are a monster, you know that?"

"Oh, I do. But gladly, I don't have a conscience," he smiled and gestured to the window. "Now watch as your people are shot out of the sky, each and every one of them."

I couldn't help but look. Craft after craft crashed, pouring chunks of flaming metal onto the city. I should have shot Michael when I had the chance. It was all my fault. I shouldn't have hesitated.

Everyone I cared for was dead, and if they weren't, they soon would be.

"Michael, I give up. Please, call them off. You've won."

"Tsk, tsk, Angela. That's not how a battle is won. You have to fight until the very end. Have you learned nothing?" He jammed the barrel of the gun into the side of my head. "Although, I cannot wait until I have the pleasure of blowing your brains out. I have been anticipating for so long, the chance to watch you die. Maybe I will be generous and kill you now so you don't have to watch the rest of the show."

"Not if I have anything to say about it," a voice came from the doorway.

I looked up to find Emmerich standing there with a dryll pointed straight at Michael. He started for us.

"You're…" I began, not able to believe that he was still alive, let alone in front of him.

"Did you think I would leave you, Angel? I knew we had a traitor, I just never thought it would be Isaac."

"Give up, Emmerich, there is no way you will win this war." Michael waved the dryll back and forth between the two of us. "Not if you want your precious Angel to survive."

"I'd rather die than let you rule!" I shouted.

"I bet you would. However…" Michael pulled me up and held me like a shield between them. "I don't think Emmerich would like that," Michael put the barrel back against my head. "Isn't that right?"

Emmerich stared at him, then dropped his dryll. "No. I wouldn't."

Michael laughed as he kicked it away from Emmerich's reach. "If it wasn't for your love for her, you probably could have taken me on. Too bad you let your emotions get the better of you. What a pair you make." He pointed the dryll at him. "Goodbye Emmerich, I will not miss you."

"No!" I elbowed Michael in the throat and shoved the dryll away from Emmerich. A shot fired toward the door, leaving a scorch mark. He dropped the dryll, and I jumped for it. Emmerich went for Michael.

I recovered it and watched as Michael and Emmerich tumbled on the ground, throwing punches and wrapping each other's hands around each other's throats. I tried to aim the dryll at Michael but I couldn't get a clear shot. They rolled out onto the balcony. Emmerich brought Michael up by the collar and punched him a few times. Michael retaliated and pulled Emmerich as they both tumbled over the edge.

"Emmerich!" I screamed, running to the ledge and looking over. They were hanging below. I reached down to Emmerich with my good hand and he grabbed ahold. With great effort, and by hooking my leg around a pillar, I got him back over the balcony.

"Are you okay?" I asked.

He nodded. "Yes, but that is the last time I fight near an open door to a balcony."

That seemed like a valid thought. I wanted to embrace him, hold him in my arms and make sure he was safe. But I couldn't rest yet.

I crawled back to the edge and reached down, ignoring Emmerich's protest. "Michael! Take my hand!"

He shook his head. "Why don't you just let me fall?"

"You know I can't do that."

He let go of the edge and I grabbed him with both hands before he could fall.

I yelled out, the pain of my broken hand resonating through my entire body.

"You are weak Angela! You bring yourself pain when you could just let me die like a true leader would!" Michael shouted.

Seeing Michael, some of the closest aircraft stopped fighting. The people on the ground were staring up at us. "Maybe a true leader would let you fall, but not a true friend."

"You were never my friend," he glanced down at the ground. "And I'm not letting you get what you want."

He shook his arm, and I lost my grip. I watched as he fell. Guards below moved out of the way as his body hit the ground.

"No!" I shouted.

"Angela, we have to hurry and stop his men before it is too late," Emmerich said.

I nodded sadly and went with him to where Markus was. He was very helpful with everything we wanted him to do, especially when he had a knife held to his throat. He called off the attack, and I watched the aircraft retreat. It was over. It was all over.

"We did it," Emmerich embraced me.

I didn't say a word, but let his warmth help me forget all that I had lost. My cousin, my people, and, at one time, my best friend.

Once people realized Michael was dead, and learned the truth about what he had done, order was restored, along with my crown. I addressed the people of Cartref; told them of my quest for peace, to end the needless loss of life on all sides, and what a worthy ally the Galaftns had been. I told them how a treaty with Galaftn could enrich

Cartrefian life. The people finally realized it was for the best and the treaty became a reality.

Emmerich was named my second-in-command, and the people erected a memorial for Elwood. I wanted everyone to remember him, the one person in my family who had stood by my side.

The sea wall was demolished, and the city began to thrive once again. As time went by, more and more hidden societies revealed themselves to Cartref. They realized I differed from my predecessors; that I stood for freedom and equality, and they didn't have to fear us anymore. I had undone the wrongs of my family. I was no longer afraid I wasn't strong enough. Peace was harder to wage than war.

Once all had calmed down, or at least what I considered being calm, Emmerich and I finally got to spend some time alone. We took that vacation to a little house my parents had owned a long time ago on the coast. I lay there on the sand, staring up at the sky as the waves touched my feet. The birds cawed in the distant.

"It's been a while since I have been on a warm beach," Emmerich said as he lay there next to me. I turned over and smiled at him.

"Oh? And when was that?" I asked.

"Not since high school, when a group of friends and I

went to Italy."

I raised an eyebrow. "A group of friends? Or some girls?"

"There was a mix of us, yes. We were all from the same school. I didn't think you would be one to get jealous, Angel."

I shoved him. "I didn't say I was jealous, I was just curious. You don't talk much about your past."

He shrugged. "There isn't much to talk about."

I watched him as he stared out into the ocean. I wondered if he was thinking about all of those people, and others, that he had left behind on Earth. His mom. His dad. They had no idea where their son had gone. They hadn't known for years now. And it was all because of me.

"You can go back, you know. We haven't destroyed the portal yet, you could go back to them," I said.

He turned to me, his eyes surprised. Emmerich shook his head. "No, I don't want to go back. Angel," he grabbed my hands and held them in his own. "I love you. Nothing changes that, I never want to lose you. Yes, I left loose ends on Earth, and yes, I miss a lot of things. But never did I imagine that in this place I would find something as extraordinary as you. You are the only thing that matters to me. You are the only one I ever want to be with."

"Emmerich, I love you too," I kissed him hard on the mouth. I cared about him with all my heart, and it brought such happiness to me he had felt the same way. "Maybe we could return and tie up those loose ends—"

He shook his head. "No, by my calculations, the next time we open a portal, it would be the last. The connection between the two worlds will disconnect and I could never return here."

"But what about your home? Can you really leave it behind?"

He placed his hand on my cheek and kissed me.

"Home is what you make it," he said.

That was when I knew I had finally found my home.

Acknowledgements

I would like to say thank you to everyone who helped me on this project, including my editor Chantelle, Justin, and Hilary, Biserka Designs for the lovely cover, and my writing group in helping me figure out where to go with this series. I would also like to thank my friends for believing in me and helping with bouncing off ideas with and reading a lot of my stories through the years. Lastly I would like to thank my parents for always supporting me and my husband who has to put up with me and all my characters.

Other works by Dani Hoots

About the Author

Dani Hoots is a science fiction, fantasy, romance, and young adult author who loves anything with a story. She has a B.S. in Anthropology, a Masters of Urban and Environmental Planning, a Certificate in Novel Writing from Arizona State University, and a BS in Herbal Science from Bastyr University.

Currently she is working on a YA urban fantasy series called Daughter of Hades, a YA urban fantasy series called The Wonderland Chronicles, a historic fantasy vampire series called A World of Vampires, and a YA sci-fi series called Sanshlian Series. She has also started up an indie publishing company called Fox Tales Press. She also works with Anthill Studios in creating comics through Antik Comics.

Her hobbies include reading, watching anime, cooking, studying different languages, wire walking, hula hoop, and working with plants. She is also an herbalist and sells her concoctions on Fox Craft Apothecary. She lives in Phoenix with her husband and visits Seattle often. Feel free to email her with any questions you might have! danihootsauthor@gmail.com.

www.ingramcontent.com/pod-product-compliance
Lightning Source LLC
Chambersburg PA
CBHW020634260626
47157CB00008B/2734